"I don't attend church

Her blood turned to ice. He

couldn't, her mind argued. She could never have fallen in love with a man who didn't love the Lord. "Why?" The one word croaked from her tight throat.

"When Mother was alive, I attended regularly. Church was important to her, so I and the rest of the family went every Sunday. But we went to please her, not because it was important to us. Only Da never went. He didn't believe in God and said on the chance he was mistaken about His existence, he wasn't about to dishonor Him by pretending to worship Him when he didn't believe."

Her chest trembled at his words. "You. . .don't believe in God?"

"I don't believe in Him or not believe in Him. If He exists, He doesn't appear to pay attention to the people He made, so I canna see that it will disturb Him if I dinna pay Him much mind."

"How can you say God doesn't take notice of us, when He sent His own Son to take the punishment for our sins?"

"I know Jesus walked this earth, but I don't know that He was the Son of God. How can I believe Jesus is God's Son, when I don't even know whether I believe God exists?"

She had no answer to that. "Does Amanda believe?"

"She feels as I do."

Carrie looked across the water, wondering that it could be so calm when she felt she was in the midst of a hurricane. Five minutes ago her world was almost perfect, and now—now everything wonderful had been ripped from her.

THE BOOK INN
2241 34th ST.
BOCK, TEXAS 79411
06) 763-6682

JOANN A. GROTE is the author of a number of popular **Heartsong Presents** historical romances. Her two-fold goal in writing fiction is to spread the message of salvation and encourage believers in their walk with Christ. Like many of her characters, JoAnn grew up in Minnesota, but she now lives with her husband in North Carolina.

Books by JoAnn A. Grote

HEARTSONG PRESENTS
HP36—The Sure Promise
HP51—The Unfolding Heart
HP55—Treasure of the Heart
HP103—Love's Shining Hope
HP120—An Honest Love
HP136—Rekindled Flame

Don't miss out on any of our super romances. Write to us at the following address for information on our newest releases and club information.

Heartsong Presents Readers' Service
P.O. Box 719
Uhrichsville, OH 44683

The Hope That Sings

JoAnn A. Grote

Heartsong Presents

A note from the Author:
I love to hear from my readers! You may write to me at the following address:

JoAnn A. Grote
Author Relations
P.O. Box 719
Uhrichsville, OH 44683

All the professional ball players appearing in *The Hope That Sings* really existed, with the exception of the hero, Dexter Riley. In addition, many of the incidents cited which include these characters actually happened.

ISBN 1-55748-870-3

THE HOPE THAT SINGS

Copyright © 1996 by JoAnn A. Grote. All rights reserved. Except for use in any review, the reproduction or utilization of this work in whole or in part in any form by any electronic, mechanical, or other means, now known or hereafter invented, is forbidden without the permission of the publisher, Heartsong Presents, P.O. Box 719, Uhrichsville, Ohio 44683.

All of the characters and events in this book are fictitious. Any resemblance to actual persons, living or dead, or to actual events is purely coincidental.

Cover illustration by Randy Hamblin.

PRINTED IN THE U.S.A.

one

St. Louis, Missouri
1882

"I must be addle-pated, Grant Chambers, accompanying you to a match game of Base Ball!" Carrie clutched her brother's arm to keep her footing in the jostling crowd. "I've always heard spectators at these matches are uncouth, and now I know it for truth."

Excitement sparkled in the eyes laughing down at her, their rich brown color so different from the blue of her own. "You won't be sorry you've come, I promise. One day you'll tell your grandchildren you saw the great Dexter Riley play for the St. Louis Browns' first American Association match. You'll love the match, you'll see, and you'll love Dexter, too. Everyone does."

She pressed closer against Grant's side, lifting her chin until it barely reached his shoulder in order to make herself better heard above the crowd. "It would be rather inappropriate for me to entertain such strong emotions toward a young man on first acquaintance. Especially a base ballist, whom everyone knows tend to be. . .ungentlemanly. I expect Emmet might object to such a reaction on my part, also."

Grant's hand cut through the air in careless dismissal. "Emmet Wilson is a good man, but he's not to be compared to the likes of Riley. Even if you are half-engaged to Wilson." His chuckle rang out. "Though I have to admit Wilson's likely better marriage material than a base ballist."

Grant had been singing the base ballist's praises since the men became friends at Washington University two years ago. Each time Grant wrote a letter home or visited her and their parents in Ridgeville, their small hometown one hundred miles to the west, Mr. Riley's name and virtues had been lavishly sprinkled throughout his conversation. The man's primary virtue was apparently his Base Ball abilities.

Grant might think a man a king simply because he could catch and strike a ball, but a man had to accomplish far more than that to win her respect, she thought. Most importantly, he had to love the Lord, as Emmet did.

The crowd of smoking, hurrying men pushed the two along toward Sportsman's Park where the match game would take place between St. Louis and Louisville.

"Oof!" A large masculine elbow barely covered by a shabby jacket sleeve caught her in the chest, and she lost her hold on Grant's arm. She stopped short, one hand pressed against the front of her garnet basque jacket, and stared at the man's back in disbelief. He hadn't even bothered to apologize!

"Hey, sister, git movin' or git out of the way." A heavily whiskered face scowled at her beneath a derby three sizes too small.

The man moved on before she could turn her sputtering protest into words, but out of sheer fear of being trampled, she took his advice.

Grant's slim hand closed about one of her elbows. "Turned around and couldn't see you for a minute. Best stick close to me."

She'd "stick" all right! Why had she ever agreed to join him?

"The Louisville club is coming!"

"Out of the way for the Eclipse club!"

Carrie looked sharply about at the crowd's calls, careful not to stop in order to do so this time. A colorful horse-drawn trolley, its warning bell clanging loudly and ineffectually, made its way through the pedestrian-filled road.

Cat calls and derisive comments concerning the Louisville club's playing ability and integrity came from every side. The base ballists returned the insults with good humor, but Carrie's face heated in shame at the crowd's rude manners.

She smiled at a wide-eyed, jaw-dropping group of boys watching the slow-moving conveyance enter Sportsman's Park. They should be involved in more edifying pursuits than Base Ball, she thought, but their misdirected hero-worship was rather amusing.

Grant grabbed her upper arm and pointed to the back of a man nearing the boys. The man wasn't overly tall, maybe five feet and eight inches; taller than her own five foot one but not as tall as Grant. The stranger was compactly built, with wide, powerful shoulders beneath his well-cut jacket. The typical black bowler covered all but a couple inches of russet brown hair that appeared neatly trimmed above the back of his collar. In one hand he carried a long, thin leather bag.

"That's him!" One of Grant's arms pierced the air. "Dexter! Over here! Over here, Riley!"

He shouldered his way through the crowd, dragging Carrie unceremoniously along behind him. When they finally reached his hero, the player was speaking to a raggedly dressed lad of about twelve. Dexter flashed Grant a smile of recognition before continuing his conversation, and Carrie had a glimpse of a pleasant wide face with smiling green eyes above a large mustache which completely hid his top lip.

His attention returned to the boy. "You here with a friend?"

The boy nodded his dirt covered face, eyes wide in awe. He pointed to a lanky boy beside him dressed as shabbily as himself.

"What's your name?"

"J—Jack."

"Here to see the match?"

Jack swallowed audibly. "Can't. Costs a quarter."

"Maybe we can strike a business deal. Could use a lad to watch over my willow while I change into my uniform, and when our club is in the field. Be worth twenty-five cents to me."

"Wow, Mister Riley! Truly?"

Riley nodded sharply. "Willing to take the job?"

"Yes sir, Mr. Riley, sir!"

Grant leaned close to Carrie's ear. "Dexter always does that. Boy carrying the bat gets into the grounds free, and the quarter lets the boy's friend join him."

A sliver of admiration slipped reluctantly into her estimation of Grant's friend.

Riley handed the bat bag and a quarter to the boy and turned to Grant, reaching to shake hands, a grin topping the wide jaw beneath the thick mustache. "Glad you could make it to the match. Did your family arrive safely?"

"Yes, thanks. Father's being interviewed this afternoon for the position with the local church I told you about, and Mother's with him. Have to be introduced to the people in charge, you know, and see whether they can pass muster. But my sister, Carrie, is with me." Grant's hand drew her forward. "This is her first match, do you believe it? Nineteen years old and never seen a Base Ball match!"

Dexter touched thick, crooked fingers to the brim of his bowler and nodded at her respectfully. Unexpectedly long lashes rayed above green eyes that kindled with sudden interest. His eyes were the color of new leaves in spring, alive with the glow of sunshine. His gaze touched the thick black hair swirled sedately beneath her bonnet, dropped to the nose—was he noticing the smattering of freckles?—before meeting her eyes again.

Carrie's gloved hand clutched the embroidered revers of her garnet basque. It felt as if her heart had simply fallen out and tumbled at his feet, right in front of his dirt-covered shoes. She barely stopped herself from glancing down to see whether she could sight it there. A laugh gurgled up within her at the fanciful thought.

And she'd believed friendship with Emmet and her high ideals made her immune to such school-girl emotions! Well, surely this inane reaction would pass, like a bad case of croup.

The admiration she saw reflected in his eyes didn't help her self-control, though she noticed her heart was back where it belonged, beating wildly against her ribs. She knew her own eyes reflected a similar admiration for him to see, but she didn't know how to hide it.

His look lingered. "I'm delighted to make your acquaintance. I hope you'll enjoy the match."

She gave him a tremulous smile. There was a pleasant hint of controlled Irish accent beneath his words. "I wish you and your club well this afternoon. I understand it's a special match game."

His smile shot into a boyish grin. His glance darted away and back again, making him appear as embarrassed as a schoolboy being teased over a girl. "Yes, well, at least to us in the clubs it's special."

She liked his modesty, liked his evident enjoyment of his work. . .if one could call playing Base Ball work.

He turned his attention back to Grant. "I'd best be getting along. I'm not even in uniform yet, and the Louisville club has already arrived."

Grant gave Dexter's shoulder a hail-fellow slap. "See you show them how Base Ball is meant to be played, old man."

Dexter's gaze darted back to her. "Why don't we join your parents at their hotel for dinner after the match, Grant?"

"They're dining with the present pastor, but Carrie and I will be available. But, say, won't you be dining with the rest of the Browns?"

His wide shoulders lifted his jacket in a nonchalant shrug. "I'll have to put in an appearance, but if it's like any normal after-match dinner, it will be primarily a liquid feast. I'll be glad for a legitimate excuse to leave early."

"We'll expect you at the Planter's Hotel, then. Say, you plan to bring your sister, don't you?"

Carrie glanced at Grant out of the corner of her eye. His question had a transparently casual tone.

Dexter's teasing grin added to her suspicion. "Expect she might be persuaded to endure your company for an evening."

His glance slipped to her face for a long moment before he turned away, making her suddenly feel it was very important to him that she be at the dinner.

"Ready, Jack?"

The boy and his friend hurried along beside him, swelling visibly at their obvious association with the man being greeted by spectators on every side as they made their way across the grounds.

She liked the way Dexter Riley carried himself, his back straight but not stiff, his wide shoulders loose, his head high, his step easy with almost a bounce to it.

She recalled the crooked fingers he had touched to his hat. "What happened to his hands, Grant? His fingers looked as if they might have been broken."

"Most of them have been broken, some more than once. Man can't play ball for years without some broken fingers. After all, nothing between their hands and a flying ball but a thin piece of leather, if that."

Ten minutes later Carrie looked down at the unpainted, backless wooden bench in distaste, holding her gray skirt away in case of dirt or snags. Was this where she was expected to spend the afternoon, on a hard piece of wood amidst a crowd of uncouth men? And these were the better seats, in the grandstand, with at least the pretense of cover in the wooden canopy overhead.

"Hey, lady, sit yerself down. Think yer made of glass? A man's gotta see the field, ya know."

Carrie sat down abruptly, and felt the wood smartly through the layers of cloth beneath her wire bustle. She couldn't remember when she'd been spoken to so rudely by so many men in one day! Were all the men in St. Louis except Grant and Mr. Riley ignorant of proper etiquette?

A man inched down the aisle six feet away, a white apron covering his trousers, one arm balancing a tray of large, amber-filled steins over his brown-and-white-striped hat which fit his fat head closely and had a brim only in the front. She wondered how he managed to keep from spilling the steins' contents with the crowd shoving him about and the tray tipping one direction and then another, like a boat on the nearby Mississippi River on a choppy day. She indicated the man to Grant. "What has he on his tray?"

Hot red color surged over Grant's narrow face. He shifted his gaze quickly to the park-like field before them. "Beer."

Carrie closed her mouth, all too aware her bottom lip had fallen in a most unbecoming manner. She touched one hand gloved in thin garnet cotton to her high-standing jacket collar. "Oh, my!"

One could as well be in a drinking establishment! And they had each paid fifty cents for the "privilege" of a hard, backless seat in the grandstand amidst a sweaty crowd of rude men on a warm May day with beer being served all about in the most open, careless manner! What would members of the congregation for which their father was being considered even this minute think if they knew? Thank the good Lord no one here would recognize her and Grant as his children!

Not that the Lord could possibly approve of their attendance, whether they were recognized or not. Her glance swept the crowded seats. There weren't more than half-a-dozen other women in the grandstand, though there were more in the cheaper, uncovered seats. Why had she ever allowed Grant to talk her into attending?

No matter why. There could be no excuse for remaining. She shot determinedly to her feet.

Grant frowned up at her. "What's wrong?"

"I'm departing."

"But the match is about to begin."

A loud roar from the stands swallowed her reply. The crowd surged to its feet. Carrie looked about, bewildered.

Grant, on his feet beside her now, grasped her arm. "The clubs are entering the grounds."

"But I mustn't stay. It's worse than I imagined."

The crowd noisily returned to its seats, and the large man behind her poked her shoulder with a blunt finger. "Look, lady, either sit yerself down or move."

She turned to leave, but a dozen large, masculine knees were between her and the aisle. She saw at least as many obstacles in the other direction. Defeated, she took her seat, her back even stiffer than her corset demanded. Surely there would be an opportunity to depart later; she'd watch for it.

The men from the Louisville club spread out across the park-like field. "They certainly present a colorful view, I shall admit that much."

Grant grunted. "Look plain silly if you ask me. American Association decided instead of the traditional club uniforms, the players would dress according to their position. For instance, the Louisville hurler is wearing that sky blue shirt."

Carrie saw the man he meant standing in the middle of the diamond-shaped ground. His belt and cap matched the silk top which laced up the front. "Hurler?"

"He tosses the ball to the batsman."

"What color does Mr. Riley wear?"

"Red and black striped. He's a center fielder. He says these uniforms won't last long. The players are already protesting them and insisting on returning to regular uniforms."

Carrie was at a loss to understand the rules of the sport. Grant spent an inordinate amount of time explaining what was happening and why, much to the fury of the man behind her. Carrie was amazed the man could hear Grant speak, for she had difficulty hearing him herself. Hollers and jeers from spectators filled the air until she thought she could see as well as hear the sound. Men hawked beer up and down the aisles. A local band played music when the clubs switched positions on the field.

She was inordinately pleased when Mr. Riley, at his first attempt as batsman, managed to run all the way around the field. His clubmates pounded him on the back, wide grins beneath their mustaches. When the clubs changed positions and Mr. Riley was playing in center field, he caught one of the flying balls, rendering the opposing batsman "out," according to Grant, and the clubs changed positions once again.

The next time Mr. Riley was batsman, the man behind her and a number of men around him rose in a roar of venomous taunts. Horrified, Carrie grasped Grant's arm and demanded an explanation. Grant's smile was wide. His brown eyes danced with unbridled excitement. "They must be from Louisville. Riley's such a good player that they're trying to upset his concentration."

"Where is their sense of justice and fair play?"

His smile only widened. "No such thing in Base Ball. Any player worth his salt can take this kind of abuse from the kranks without it affecting his play."

"Kranks?"

Grant's hand waved casually while he turned his attention back to the field, where Riley stood beside the white rubber square. "Male spectators are called kranks. Ladies are kranklets."

A high-pitched "thunk" sounded when Riley's bat struck the ball. It flew straight above him, and came down between him and a man Grant called the catcher. The catcher tossed the ball back to the hurler, and Riley took up the batsman's normal stance.

The crowd surged to their feet again, their roar increasing.

Disgusted, Carrie rose, too, weaving her head back and forth, attempting to view the field through the people.

Beside her, Grant cupped freckled hands about his lips. "Murder the ball, Riley!"

The man behind them shoved a huge hand against Grant's shoulder. "Hey, what's the big idea, rootin' fer the Browns?"

Imagine this loud, uncouth man upbraiding them for supporting their friend! Just as though this wasn't America, where one might speak one's own mind. Or yell one's own sentiments at a ball park. Her fists settled momentarily where her tailored basque covered her hips. She glared into the ruddy, bewhiskered face towering above her. "We shall call for whomever we please, sir!"

Turning about, she cupped her gloved hands delicately about her own mouth and rather timidly repeated Grant's call.

Grant burst out in pure laughter. Carrie flushed.

A loud crack sounded through the park, and she saw the ball whiz across the field. Riley hurtled toward the first sandbag, his powerful legs in their knee-high brown socks pumping madly.

All decorum fell away. "Run, Mr. Riley, run!" she screamed.

By the time Dexter Riley was back at the Home Base, Carrie's throat was sore from the strain of its unaccustomed use, Dexter's clubmates were leaping about him like a group of uniformed frogs, and the kranks behind her were using language more colorful than the clubs' uniforms. She felt an immense satisfaction at Dexter's accomplishment, and her own choice to cheer him on.

two

It was considerate of Dexter to choose the hotel at which she and her parents were staying to have dinner, Carrie thought later in her hotel room, looking through the few outfits she'd brought for the week they expected to be in the city. Dexter's choice gave her the opportunity to refresh herself and change into a proper gown for the evening, and she did need the opportunity after a day at the ball grounds!

What would her mother and father say when they discovered her afternoon outfit smelling like beer from the stein the man behind them had spilled upon her? Most likely he had poured it upon her by choice rather than accident, she thought angrily, pulling the stained, tailored skirt over the small wire bustle with difficulty.

She hesitated only slightly before selecting a favorite gown of ice-blue satin for the evening, its basque-like top trimmed with deep white lace, which met in a point beneath the large satin bow attached just over the understated bustle. The double-rows of matching lace trimming the wrists were set off with tiny satin bows of deepest sapphire, as was the high collar. The ivory-colored slippers with raised embroidery of the same shade felt wonderfully light after the sensible, high-topped, brown leather shoes she'd worn that afternoon.

Using the large mirror topping the low, two-drawer bureau to place faux-pearl studded combs in her swirl of black hair, she had to admit the gown was a decided improvement over the functional garnet basque and gray skirt she'd worn to Sportsman's Park. She well knew the ice-blue was one of her most flattering dresses, setting off both her coloring and figure to advantage, yet demure enough to be considered proper for a lady, and a reverend's daughter at that. What would Dexter Riley think of her in the gown?

Mr. Riley's thoughts were no concern of hers, she reminded herself for the dozenth time while closing the door to the room and entering the spacious, carpeted hallway. *I am simply dining with my brother and his friends. It's not as though Mr. Riley is calling upon me. I'd never betray Emmet in such a manner.*

Still, she was looking forward to spending the evening with one of the city's most popular young men of the day. She was sure the afternoon's match had been much more exciting because she'd met one of the men involved. It thrilled her that Dexter's St. Louis Browns won the match nine runs to seven. She couldn't wait to congratulate him for his excellent play.

Not that her heart was threatened by this lively young man with the wonderful smile and laughing eyes, she hastened to assure herself, discounting her initial reaction to him.

But when Dexter and his sister met them in the lobby minutes later, her heart performed the same dropping act it had performed upon meeting him earlier in the day. Dismay swept through her at its betrayal of her commitment to Emmet.

As though she had any reason to be concerned that she might have an opportunity to be unfaithful! If the rumors she'd heard about base ballists were true, women fell all over themselves for the privilege of their company. Not the type of women a gentleman would court, of course. Still, it was unlikely Mr. Riley would single her out for attention, in spite of the respectful admiration which glowed so plainly in his eyes.

He was devastatingly handsome in a silver-gray dress coat and crisp white linen shirt front with gray silk jabot. The formal attire couldn't hide the wide shoulders that had filled the red-and-black striped base ballist's shirt that afternoon, nor the power that lay beneath the civilized linen shirt. Yet he didn't act like a man aware of the attention he drew, and she found him all the more appealing for his attitude.

His hair was no longer hidden by the bowler he'd worn when they met or the brown-and-white striped hat he'd worn while playing. *It's wonderful hair*, she thought, *thick and shiny, its brown color richly steeped in wine-red.*

She liked his sister immediately, and wasn't surprised to find they were twins. Amanda had her brother's coloring, her eyes as clear a peridot green. Her thick hair, the same wonderful shade as Dexter's, glowed in the light of the chandeliers, and was wound in a smooth figure eight covering the back of her head. Jade-tipped tortoiseshell hairpins studded the waves. The emerald swirled silk she wore added to her beauty. Like Dexter, she was quick to smile and laugh, and had a pleasant manner which casually shunned compliments directed toward herself, and pursued only the kindest of topics involving others. Carrie hoped they would become friends if her father accepted the position with the church in this city.

If Grant's devoted attention to Amanda was any indication, she would have every opportunity to meet the girl again!

But Carrie couldn't avoid paying attention to Dexter by observing his sister too long. Dexter gave her his arm on which to enter the dining room, and his warm smile started a curling tingle in her stomach. She fervently hoped the lighting flattered her as well as it did Amanda.

Not that anyone else would notice. A number of patrons stopped the couple on their way to the table, but she received only brief glances. Everyone's attention was focused upon Dexter, one of the nine young men who had made the city proud that day.

Only moments after they were seated, Dexter asked if she'd enjoyed the match game that afternoon.

"Did she enjoy it? I'll tell the world she enjoyed it!" Grant answered for her. "It was a sight to make a brother proud. She may have been a novice this afternoon, but this evening she's the Browns' most ardent kranklet."

Carrie's cheeks warmed at Grant's comments and she lowered her gaze. "I would hardly call myself a— "

"You should have seen have seen her, Dexter," he continued on as though she hadn't spoken. "Man behind us was so large he looked like he wore a barrel beneath his vest. His hands could meet about a ripe watermelon. Had a face like a storm cloud. Tried to make me stop cheering you on, but he didn't frighten Carrie a bit. She told him in no uncertain terms that this was America, and a person could support whomever they chose. And then she yelled so loud for you to whack that ball that she drowned out all the kranks sitting about us."

Carrie busily brushed an imaginary speck of dirt from the lace at her wrist. "You are exaggerating, much to the detriment of my reputation. I admit supporting Mr. Riley's efforts, but I certainly did not suggest that he 'whack' the ball, nor could I possibly have called louder than those monstrous, coarse men sitting about us, even if I had wished to do so." Shooting him an indignant look, she caught him winking at Dexter, his grin wide, and her mortification increased.

Dexter's large, firm fingers touched her wrist briefly, drawing her averted gaze to his. "I'm honored you championed me and my club, Miss Carrie. I've no doubt you did in a proper manner."

She expected to see a sarcastic grin on his handsome face in spite of the respectful tone in his voice. There was none. Still, she was convinced he was silently laughing at her along with Grant. "Is your brother a man to be trusted, Amanda? For I give you fair warning, Grant is not!"

Amanda laughingly ignored Grant's sputtering protest. "You'll know when to distrust Dexter, for when he starts peddling the blarney, an Irish accent fills his speech." She tipped her head slightly, observing her brother with sparkling eyes. "The same thing happens when he's angry. He never raises his voice or his fists, but he slips into our grandparents' manner of speaking."

Carrie shared a blatantly conspiratorial look with Amanda, then glanced teasingly at Dexter. "I'll remember that. An Irish accent means his words are blarney."

His green eyes twinkled. "No fair! How am I to know when you are kissing the blarney stone?"

"Why, I'm surprised at you, sir. A true gentleman never finds a woman's behavior deceiving, only charmingly mysterious."

Dexter's laugh rang out at her nonsense.

But moments later when two young couples stopped to congratulate him on the day's ball match and she turned her attention back to Grant and Amanda, she was surprised to see her brother watching her with a puzzled frown. Did he think her too flirtatious with his friend?

When the base ballist's admirers left them, she was quieter and more reserved at first, but it wasn't long before Dexter had her laughing again with the rest of the party with tales of antics pulled on trips with ball clubs throughout the midwestern and eastern states. She'd never known anyone who traveled so extensively and often, and it made his acquaintance even more exciting.

Grant apparently forgot his concern for her, also. He laughed and joked along with the rest of them, but he had eyes only for Amanda. Carrie soon realized the two had the comfortable atmosphere between them that spoke of many past hours together.

Well, Amanda seemed a lovely woman, intelligent and charming. If she could bring that devoted look to her brother's eyes—and hopefully devotion to his heart as well—Carrie could only hope Amanda returned his affections.

"I've rented a carriage," Dexter announced casually while they were finishing bowls of lemon-flavored ice cream. "Since Carrie hasn't seen the city, I thought we might show her how it looks at night from the Bridge."

Carrie lectured herself sternly while retrieving her elbow-length cape from her room, telling herself she must maneuver it so she sat with Amanda in the carriage. But when the four reached the rented conveyance, Grant handed Amanda carefully into the rear seat and stepped immediately up beside her, for all the world as though he hadn't felt Carrie's restraining hand on his forearm or heard her offer to join Amanda. There was nothing left for Carrie but to sit beside Dexter.

She lifted her skirt with one hand in preparing to enter, giving Dexter a slight smile. She hoped he hadn't heard her intention to sit beside his sister and been insulted by it. Of course, there had been nothing said by any party indicating the two of them were to consider themselves coupled for the evening, but even so. . .

She was uncomfortably aware of him sitting beside her, their bodies swaying slightly with the motion of the carriage, and she held herself quite rigid at first. It wasn't long before Dexter's casual manner in pointing out St. Louis' attractions relaxed her, though it was difficult to appreciate the architecture in the gas-lit night. She knew that Fourth Street, where the hotel was located, catered to the wealthy elite, and a number of buildings were quite magnificent. It was all very different from the small town of Ridgeville.

Dexter sprinkled bits of history into his tour, telling how the French settled the area and named it over one hundred years earlier, to be followed by the Spanish, and, in the middle to late part of the current century, by large contingents of German and Irish immigrants.

"That last is how Amanda and I arrived here." He laughed at himself. "Or more accurately, how our grandparents arrived. We made our appearances much later."

"Did your grandparents come over during the potato famine?"

"Yes. My mother's and father's parents were friends. They came over on the same boat, eventually settling here. My mother was ten at the time, my father fourteen."

"I've heard stories of the famine, awful tales of what people endured both in Ireland and on the emigration boats. I'm sorry your parents and grandparents experienced it."

"Their life improved after they settled here."

She unconsciously smoothed the gloves over the back of her hands. "When I consider what some people suffer, I think I've not been tried at all by life."

Though most of his face was shadowed by the night and the brim of his formal high hat, she saw his smile blaze down, throwing her heart into that uncomfortable, wonderful frenzy. "You're not so ancient. Take heart! Life's hurler might throw a couple trying experiences your direction yet."

She laughed with him. "You are quite correct. Anything might happen!"

He turned the conversation away from problems and continued his comments on the buildings they passed. She found his enthusiasm for his home contagious; she'd like to be part of this city, and hoped her father would take the position if offered him. Of course, her life wouldn't be cast with her parents for long. When she married Emmet, her place would be beside him, wherever he chose to live.

Her mind skittered away from the suddenly uncomfortable thought.

They entered one end of the bridge and Carrie gasped. "I didn't realize it was so large! I believe three or four carriages could meet easily."

"This bridge is considered one of the engineering wonders of the world."

Lights along each side stretched the entire length of the bridge, above high wrought iron railings, creating a shining corridor beneath the sky's black dome. Carrie found the effect breathtaking.

Dexter halted the carriage where the bridge formed a baylike outcropping. A bench waited patiently in the mellow rays from a large gas lamp for someone to settle himself down and enjoy the view. The Mississippi River lay in a long, wide black ribbon, but Carrie could hear the water lapping against the great pillar beneath them. Rippling gold reflected the lights of passing ferries, barges, and steamboats. Along the banks of the river and the rolling lands behind, lights from the city burned through a foggy haze. Dexter explained the haze was the city's constant companion from the riverside industries which depended upon the water-road for their survival.

Her gaze locked with Dexter's when he helped her from the carriage, sending her heart on another wild gallop. When her delicate evening slippers stood securely upon the bridge, he tucked her gloved hand beneath his arm in as natural a manner as if they'd been promenading together for years. She tried to act as casual as he did, not wishing him to know his effect on her.

Grant and Amanda joined them after a moment. The four of them crowded companionably on the wrought iron bench, making the usual comments about the weather and the view. Yet it seemed wildly romantic to Carrie, seated snugly between Dexter and Amanda, Dexter's hand still resting intimately upon hers.

Others were out enjoying the warm evening air, and Amanda told her the bridge was a popular place for young couples. The identification of the bridge as a trysting spot awakened again the disturbing feeling that she was betraying Emmet's trust, and Carrie gently removed her hand from Dexter's arm.

A breeze from the river played with her cape, and she was glad she'd taken time to put on her best bonnet. The wide ribbon of ivory satin was tied in a huge, soft bow at one side of her chin, framing her face in addition to securing the bonnet against the wind. The admiration she saw in Dexter's eyes let her know he found the picture appealing.

She exclaimed in delight when the unexpected music of an exquisite Viennese waltz filled the night. The four of them rushed to stand along the railing. The steamboat from which the music came slid from beneath the span near them, people promenading and dancing along the gaily illuminated decks.

Dexter swept off his high top hat with a flourish and bowed deeply. "May I have the honor of this dance?"

Before she thought to decline, she was in his arms, his strength whirling her about with unexpected grace. He didn't hold her tightly, but the intimacy of their contact momentarily erased the rest of the world for her, and there was nothing but the exquisite freedom of moving with him to the music, the compelling wonder of the smiling green eyes whose gaze never left her own. His cologne wafted in and out of the wild smell of the river and the stringent lingering of smoke from the boats below, forming an invisible, fragrant fence around the little world that included only the two of them. She enjoyed the energy Dexter generated as much as the dance itself. Emmet would never act in such an impromptu manner; he always weighed any possible consequences before acting.

It was the sight of Grant taking Amanda in his arms to join them in the dance that brought her to her senses. She'd only danced twice in her life, both times at wedding receptions, and couldn't recall ever seeing Grant dance. Obviously the entertainment was not new to him, she thought, watching the way he expertly turned Amanda. She wondered where he had become so skilled. Their parents discouraged dancing. Her father believed it encouraged young men to take inappropriate liberties with their partners and to believe their partners would welcome such liberties.

Laughter and applause of approval from a passing carriage brought Carrie's feet to a halt, almost tripping Dexter in her suddenness. He released her without comment when she stepped back from his arms, but she had more difficulty releasing her gaze from his. "The music is ending," she explained breathlessly.

The music was indeed fading down the river. Carrie leaned against the cool metal railing, watching the boat with its gay passengers move into the night, the paddlewheel at its rear as busy as the bustle on a large-hipped woman.

Grant and Amanda had drifted a few yards up the bridge. Carrie saw that they, too, had stopped dancing, but Amanda remained in his arms. As she watched, he bent his head and kissed her.

Carrie jerked her gaze away. She hadn't intended to spy on them. It wasn't as though Grant was toying with Amanda, she argued with the part of her conscience that accused him. He couldn't so much as look at the vivacious young woman without revealing his love for her. Yet she wished he would show more discretion than to kiss her in such a public place, even though darkness covered them from all but the nearest passing carriages.

Beside her at the railing, Dexter shifted his weight, and his arm came to rest lightly against hers. She went completely still, her heart pounding wildly, staring out at the midnight blackness of the river. Had he seen Grant and Amanda's embrace? She didn't dare look at him. What if he tried to kiss her? Should she have taken Amanda's laughing reference to the bridge as a local lovers' lane seriously? Did a man consider it an invitation to improper advances if a girl allowed herself to be escorted here?

Surely not! Grant would never have allowed her to come, would never have left her to Dexter's escort, if such a thing were true. The realization gave her a sense of relief, though she was still overly conscious of Dexter's presence.

Yet she couldn't help wondering what Dexter's kiss would be like.

She was relieved when Amanda and Grant rejoined them.

Moments later, an unusually loud, raucous, unladylike laugh jolted her thoughts toward two couples making their way unsteadily toward them. There was nothing improper about the women's attire, but their manner was entirely unseemly. Each leaned against one of the men for support, and the men leaned back upon the women. For every step forward, they took three weaving stumbles back.

The women's obviously drunken state so horrified Carrie that she barely noticed the men until Dexter said quietly, "It's Browning and Mullane, Grant."

Carrie recoiled from his words. Surely her brother and Mr. Riley could not be on familiar terms with these intoxicated people!

Her brother muttered something beneath his breath. Dexter walked around the bench to intercept the staggering foursome.

three

The drunken men greeted Dexter exuberantly. Carrie flinched when the tallest one stumbled against him, leaning heavily on his shoulder. He burped loudly in Dexter's face. "Riley, old man, good ta see ya! Want ta join us in a liddle li. . .liba. . .in a drink?" He held an open bottle toward him.

"Think you've had enough, Mullane. If you plan to beat us on the grounds tomorrow, you'd best be hitting the sack instead of the bottle."

"Huh! Think just 'cause your ol' Browns skinned by us today we can't whip ya tomorra!"

Dexter grinned. "'Skinned' by you? We walked away with the match! Why, Browning here didn't manage a single hit in the four times he came to the plate!"

The man named Browning leaned forward, wagging a finger beneath Dexter's nose. "Jest didn't have the right encouragement." He kissed the girl beside him with a loud smack that sent the blood rushing to Carrie's cheeks. "Now thet's encouragement."

Disappointment drained the joy from Carrie at the realization Dexter counted these men among his friends.

Mullane peered over Dexter's shoulder at the bench, and Carrie wished she could simply step over the edge of the bridge and disappear beneath the wide expanse of black water. "Thet Amanda over there? Why, sure is! Browning, it's Amanda! How ya doin', sweet thing?"

She was amazed to hear Amanda's bubbling laughter as he brushed past Dexter, stumbling heavily against the bench. Grant reached out quickly to keep him from falling. The man was remarkably good looking, Carrie noted, or would have been if he'd been sober. His jacket, on the other hand, was outdated, and looked as if it would fall apart at the seams at the slightest provocation.

A watery grin appeared beneath Mullane's thin black mustache. "Why, it's Chambers! Didn't recognize you at first. 'Course, I had my eye on the ladies, ya understand." Carrie was sure his exaggerated wink was meant to be conspiratorial. "Who's this lovely creature aside ya?"

"No one you need to know," Dexter said, grasping the man's shoulders from behind and pulling him back. "Where's your buggy?"

Mullane squinted toward one end of the bridge, then pointed. "Thataway. Somewhere." The hand with the bottle went up to his forehead in an impossible attempt to scratch his head. His derby flew over the wrought iron railing and drifted from sight, revealing the thickest black wavy hair Carrie had ever seen on a man. He leaned against the top of the railing, raised his thick brows, and peered over. "Oops."

The woman with him laughed hysterically. Browning, his own derby resting safely on top of his large ears, looked down at the river. "It's gone, old man."

Dexter slipped one of Mullane's arms over his shoulders. "You two need to get back to your hotel. Wouldn't want your owner or the press to see you in this condition, what with a match tomorrow."

Grant stood up with a sigh. "Don't care to leave Amanda and Carrie alone while we escort these two yahoos to their buggy, so I guess I'd better retrieve their buggy while you wait with the ladies."

"I'll have to see them back to their hotel."

"Aw, Dex, you don't have to do any such thing." Grant protested. "Don't let them spoil our evening. It's not your responsibility these two are painting the town."

"They're my friends." His voice was low, but brooked no argument. "Besides, it isn't good for Base Ball for players to be found in this kind of shape."

"The public knows good and well the way most base ballers live, but you're bound and determined to be honorable about it, I'll see them back to their lodgings. Suspicious as base ballers are about each others' clubs, wouldn't surprise me if you were accused of getting these two drunk to better the Browns' chances tomorrow, should you be seen with them."

"Hadn't thought of that. I suppose you're right."

"'Course I'm right."

"Hate to leave the job to ye, though."

"Don't see anyone else here to do it. Those two ladies hanging on their arms sure aren't going to be an asset in the situation. Since you're one of the few base ballers who doesn't drink, falls to you all too often to look after your mates. Besides, someone has to see Carrie and Amanda back safely." His gaze lingered on Amanda before he turned toward Mullane and Browning, taking a deep breath as he did so, as if fortifying himself against an unpleasant task, which Carrie could well imagine he thought it.

At least she was glad to hear Dexter apparently took no part in his friends' manner of recreation.

When Grant had retrieved the men's conveyance, and he and Dexter had loaded the four wobbly passengers into it, he drove off.

Amanda patted gloved fingertips lightly against her lips to hide a yawn. "I hate to admit to being a social disaster, Carrie, but I'm afraid I won't be able to stay awake on the drive back. Would you mind awfully keeping my brother company?"

What choice had she but to defer to Amanda's wishes and join Dexter once again in the front seat of the open carriage? She tried to deny the ribbon of joy that floated inside her at spending more time intimately at his side.

They hadn't gone far before he cleared his throat. "I'm sorry your evening had to end this way. I wish your first evening with. . .in St. Louis could have been perfect."

"It's been a lovely evening. But. . .will Grant be safe with those men?"

"Of course, he will." She wondered whether he was trying to convince himself as well as her. "Mullane and Browning aren't so bad when they've not been drinking. I played with Browning on the Louisville club before Von der Ahe signed me up for the Browns. I'd probably have stayed with Louisville if St. Louis wasn't my hometown. Anyway, Browning and I joined Louisville the same time, five years ago now, when we were fifteen."

She knew a number of young men who supported themselves at that age, but not as base ballers!

"Mullane, now," Dexter was continuing, "he's some terrific hurler. Helped me improve my throw."

"You plan to abandon center field to become a hurler?" She couldn't help the bit of pride she felt in recalling his position.

He laughed good-naturedly. "No. I'll never be good enough at it to be a hurler."

"Is Browning a hurler?"

"No, but he's got the stuff to make one of the top hitters of our day, if he'll just stay off the liquor. It was Browning told me it's nearly worth a player's career what willow he chooses."

"Willow?"

"Bat. Most clubs keep a supply of willows, and the players choose from among them when it's their turn as batsman. But Browning says if a man uses the same willow long enough, he gets used to the feel of it, knows exactly what he can do with it, ups the percentage that he'll hit any hurler's ball. That's why I carry my own willow to each match game, though most players think I'm a fool for going to the trouble and expense of it." He shrugged slightly. "I tried Mullane's suggestions and tried Browning's advice, and sure enough if my playing didn't improve. I'll never be as good as either of them, but I'm consistent, and for many ball club owners, that's worth a lot."

They turned on to a narrower street, and Dexter gave his attention to keeping the horses in line when they met a carriage coming from the opposite direction. Picking up where he'd left off, he said, "Suppose Base Ball is like any business. Only room for so many men to make a living at it, so players are pretty stingy with advice. Figure I owe a lot to Mullane and Browning."

"Are you always so loyal to your friends?"

He shifted his shoulders, keeping his gaze on the street. Was he uncomfortable at her mention of his virtue? Did he think her amused by it? "It is an admirable quality," she assured him quietly.

A moment later they turned another corner. "We're almost to the Planter's." A few paces further he opened his mouth, shut it, then tried again. "I was wondering, would ye. . .that is, is there for being any reason I couldn't. . .or ye wouldn't. . .I mean, would ye be for allowing me to call on ye while ye be in the city?" he finished with a rush.

She was touched by his uncharacteristic stumbling, and the broadening of his Irish accent, which she recalled Amanda insisting happened only when he was speaking blarney or was upset. She didn't think he was teasing now, and he wasn't angry, so he must be nervous. Imagine a well-known base ballist nervous at asking to call on a small-town preacher's daughter!

Her sympathetic amusement fled at the memory of Emmet. "I. . .I am being courted by a young man back home."

He said nothing, only stared ahead. She wished it were day so she could see his expression. It would help if he would even remove his stovepipe, as its brim deepened the shadows over his face.

"I. . .his name is Emmet. Emmet Wilson."

She heard him swallow. "Ye say he is courting ye, but haven't said that ye've promised yourself to him."

The simple statement sent her thoughts into confusion. Had she not said so because her heart refused to acknowledge such a thing in his presence? She could say it now, and never see Dexter Riley again. It was the honorable thing to do. She would say it to any other man; she had said it to a number of them.

She felt as much as saw him turn toward her. "Carrie?"

The word was spoken softly. Only one word, but she heard

the hope expressed in it, and it was that hope to which she responded. "I've made no promise to him in words, nor has he asked me to do so."

"Then, may I call?"

"I don't wish to mislead you. Emmet is. . .I'm very fond of him. We've been close since we were children. I never thought of. . ." she broke off, embarrassed. Dexter had simply asked whether he might call on her. How could she, in reply, say she'd never considered marriage to anyone but Emmet? That in spite of her desire to see Dexter again—and she wished to do so desperately—she was sure she would still marry Emmet?

They stopped in front of the hotel entrance. A uniformed hotel employee held their horses while Dexter assisted her down. His hands remained lightly at her waist, his rich brown eyes still asking the question, though he didn't repeat it.

"I don't know how long we'll be in the city."

He must have recognized her comment for the permission to call on her that it was meant, for his smile blazed across his face and shone from his eyes in a joy that humbled her.

"We play Louisville again tomorrow afternoon. I won't be able to call until the match is over. Perhaps you will be among the spectators?"

Did the eagerness in his question mean he wanted her there? "I don't know. Grant may have classes, and I doubt my father would escort me." It wouldn't be proper to go unescorted, of course, nor would she dare to do so, considering the manner of people to which she'd been exposed among the spectators today.

"Then, if at all possible, I'll be here by seven tomorrow evening."

His look was so ardent, she had to glance away, but she thrilled to it nonetheless. She nodded and hurried toward the door.

Three paces from the entrance she whirled back around. "Oh, Mr. Riley!"

Her words weren't spoken loudly, nor did they need to be, for she saw with pleasant confusion that he was still standing beside the carriage, watching her. He stepped toward her eagerly. "Yes?"

One hand clutched the top of her cape, where the black velvet frog secured it. "I forgot to wish you well in the match game tomorrow."

His smile brought a trembling one from her before she went inside. She resisted the urge to turn about once more for a last look at his dear face.

Tomorrow. Tomorrow she'd see him again. Less than twenty-four hours.

Anticipation put wings on her ivory satin slippers as she crossed the thickly carpeted foyer to the ornate elevator that would take her to her floor.

❧

Best day of his life.

Since attending his first match game of Base Ball at the age of five, Dexter had had only one goal: to be a base baller, and a good one. When he signed the contract with the Louisville club five years ago, he'd thought he'd never again feel so heady over anything.

But today left that accomplishment in the dust. Today, for the first time, he'd played in a season game for a major league club, played well, and his club had won. One couldn't expect life to get better than this.

But it had. Better than a shut-out against your ball club's worst rival.

He'd met Carrie.

There wasn't a doubt in his mind that she was the woman for him, for the rest of his life and then some. He clasped his hands behind his head and stared out the window beside his bed at the stars trying to shine through the constant factory-smoke haze camouflaging the St. Louis skies. The grin that had barely left his face all day stretched wider.

She was a beauty, Carrie was. Known Grant for two years, and not once had the fellow told him how beautiful she was. 'Course, being her brother, he wouldn't be likely to notice.

Though it was beyond him how even a brother could be blind to skin that glowed like a dogwood blossom in moonlight, framed by hair that shimmered as sleekly black as the Mississippi River at night.

He lifted his hands, their twenty-year-old knuckles already permanently swollen from injuries received catching base balls, and examined their lumpy silhouettes against the light of night coming through the window, imagining the softness of her hair against his tough, callused skin.

He let his hands fall back to his sides, picturing her face as he'd first seen it. He loved the way the unexpected cocker-brown freckles sprinkled across the tiny bridge of her nose and beneath her blue eyes. Couldn't be more than a dozen of the things. He'd count those freckles the next time he saw her, indeed he would.

His laugh rang out bright and clear at the thought, and his boardingmate, who played first base, snorted and rolled over at the sound. Dexter closed his grinning lips hard together. He and his boardingmate had made a good play that day, a perfect play, smart, sharp, efficient, putting a Louisville player out at third. His hands stung yet at the remembrance of catching that fly, for the player was a slugger of the first degree, though not normally as good as Browning.

The joy in his chest tempered somewhat at the thought of Browning. One of the best base ballers he'd ever seen play, but the man would drink as many nickel pails of beer as a person could line up in front of him. Only thing that kept this day from being perfect was Browning and Mullane putting on that disgusting display in front of Carrie. Didn't take much to see she wasn't accustomed to men in such condition.

Of course, one would expect a preacher's daughter to be protected from the world. Likely she felt as strongly about God as Grant, who often urged him to try trusting Christ. Dexter didn't know many other men who felt so strongly about their religion.

Well, he liked an attitude of reverence toward God in a woman. The women who followed the base ballers didn't mind a man who drank, or used coarse language, or told unseemly stories in their presence, or stole a few kisses—or made more improper advances. He enjoyed the heady feeling a woman's attention gave any man, but he refused to take advantage of the silly creatures, even if they didn't appear to mind being compromised.

Least of all did such women consider God important. Not that he could condemn them for that. He hadn't much use for God himself. He didn't even know whether he believed in Him or not. God, if He did exist, didn't appear to take much interest in men, not that he could notice, anyway. And he'd seen men who professed faith who were as base as those who openly shunned religion. Of course, there were a few men of faith who seemed sincere—men like Grant. He supposed Carrie would prefer such a man.

Carrie. He folded his hands behind his head and grinned. Guess he might as well get used to her keeping him company in his mind. Only thing that came near to being as pleasant to think on was a perfect play like he and his roommate had made today, or an uncatchable hit with three of your clubmates on base.

Those delicate black eyebrows of hers were as pretty as a base ball in flight, and just as deceiving. A wrapped ball flying through the air didn't look like it could pack a powerful wallop, any more than a man would suspect the things an innocent raising of those eyebrows could do to his stomach.

And she'd granted him permission to see her tomorrow evening.

Yes sir, it had been a pert'-near perfect day. Best day of his life.

four

Carrie didn't attend the match the next day. Dexter's team lost, but he didn't appear disconcerted. He was as entertaining as he'd been the previous evening. Her parents and Grant joined them for dinner, and she was delighted to see her parents liked the young man as well as she and Grant did.

With ruddy cheeks, he'd presented both Carrie and Mrs. Chambers flowers he'd purchased from the raggedy flower girls who filled the street to earn a few pennies in front of the hotel from dawn to sunset.

"They aren't the city's finest flowers, but--" He'd shrugged and left the explanation unfinished.

But she knew he meant no slight to her and her mother. Rather his kind heart went out to the children in their poverty as it had to the boys he allowed into the ball grounds without damaging their pride. She liked him the more for it but didn't diminish his kind act by saying so, or by telling him she purchased a bouquet for her room daily. Instead, she pinned the most delicate blossom to her gown, and sent a maid to her room with the rest. She was pleased when her mother did the same.

She and Dexter didn't go riding or promenading after dinner, but spent the evening in the elegant lobby. The hours went by too quickly as they grew better acquainted, liking each other more with each bit of knowledge, eagerly drinking in the way the other looked, the unique timber of their voices, seeing their growing admiration and affection for each other reflected in each other's eyes.

Her mother protested slightly the next day when Carrie told her Dexter would be joining her for the third evening in a row, but Carrie assured her there could be nothing amiss in spending time with Grant and his friend, and the older women was appeased for the moment.

That evening Dexter, Carrie, and Grant attended a play together at Washington University. Amanda had a small role in the play, and she performed her part admirably with an appealing energy that won the audience's whole-hearted approval. Carrie enjoyed spending the hours beside Dexter, sharing glances during the performance, and discovering with delight that they laughed at the same things. Often their gazes would catch and mingle in the dim light, and they would forget the play until the laughter of those around them rang out and brought their gazes back to the stage.

Toward the middle of the last act, Dexter rested his hand over hers. She darted a surprised look at his face, her heart pattering explosively in her chest and ears. When she didn't pull her hand away, he smiled at her; not the usual, easy-going smile that seldom seemed to leave his face, or the friendly smile he gave admirers who approached him, but a smile warmed with something akin to devotion. She turned her gaze back to the stage, but her attention remained with the large, rather disfigured, callused hand that claimed her own, and the eyes that held the suggestion of a whole new world.

As usual, a number of people in the audience recognized Dexter, and Carrie waited patiently while they stopped to speak with him after the play. A few asked him to autograph their programs, which he did, laughingly commenting that it was the performers who should be signing. In their eagerness to get close to the popular base ballist, some of the crowd pushed their way between Carrie and Dexter. Carrie stepped back to give them way, but Dexter, smilingly excusing himself to the responsible parties, drew her back to his side.

The action caught the attention of the onlookers, who eyed her curiously. Some of the young women gazed at her boldly, their looks accusing her of being where she had no right. One of the female admirers rested a glove on Dexter's other arm, leaning against him and smiling alluringly into his face. He responded respectfully to her gushing compliments and moved discreetly in such a manner that her hand was forced to slip away.

Carrie, accustomed to life in a small community, found it a heady experience to be escorted by someone so readily recognized and admired, to say nothing of a man whose company was sought after by women in such a forward manner. Still, though the experience was exhilarating, it wasn't his perhaps temporary fame which caused her to enjoy his company so much. It was the man himself she enjoyed, she thought, watching him discreetly while they drove together later through Lafayette Park in the one-seat open carriage.

She had been dismayed when Grant informed them he and Amanda had made their own plans after the play, but she agreed eagerly to Dexter's offer of a drive.

It was a beautiful spring evening, with clear skies which appeared almost bright from the light of the surrounding city. The upper-class community was far enough from the river that it escaped the city's industrial haze, and a handful of scattered stars dotted the sky. The slight breeze carried the scent of new leaves, which blended with the mixture of leather from the carriage and reins, the horses, and her own violet scent.

Dexter pulled the horse to a gentle stop alongside a small lake, across which the emerging moon cast a wavering path, catching the shimmering veil of water from a man-made fountain in its midst. Carrie caught her breath at the sight, leaning forward slightly. "How lovely!"

"Sometime I'll bring you here during the day, when you can see it well. We'll take a small skiff out, and row to the island."

He wanted to continue seeing her! The wonder of it made her speechless.

He lifted his eyebrows and grinned. "Difficult to find time to spend with you during daylight hours, though. The afternoons we don't have a match game scheduled, we have practice."

She wanted to ask whether they couldn't come to the park on Sunday afternoon, but the suggestion was too bold, so she said instead, "I'd like to attend another of your matches before we leave for Ridgeville."

He dropped his gaze to his fingers, which played idly with the reins. "Your father probably doesn't approve of Base Ball, or of base ballers."

She replied to the true question she suspected buried in his statement. "He has expressed no disapproval of you. On the contrary, he told Grant what a fine young man he believed you to be, and that he was glad Grant had found such a friend here."

He turned his face to her. "And has your father commented on my escorting you?"

She hoped he couldn't see her flush in the darkness. "My parents have no objection to my assisting Grant in entertaining his friends."

He didn't respond immediately. Only the stirring of the horse in its harness broke the silence until he said, "Some people are embarrassed to associate with base ballers. I know a player who changed his name when he joined a professional ball club, so as not to bring disgrace on his family." He hesitated, and when he spoke again, his voice was low. "Are you ashamed to be escorted by me, Carrie?"

The pain in his voice resonated through her. "Never!" She leaned toward him in a spontaneous gesture, resting her hand on his forearm and looking up into his face. "I'm proud to be escorted by you. Not because of your profession, but because of the type of man you are: kind and compassionate and loyal and fine and—"

"Carrie!" Her name barely left his lips before he'd drawn her close and covered her mouth with his. The kiss was warm and lingering, and she thought only of how wonderful it was, how different from Emmet's brotherly kisses.

And even the memory of Emmet didn't cause her to draw away from Dexter's embrace.

"I was afraid ye could never care for me." His breath fanned her cheek with his cracked whisper.

Tumultuous joy bubbled through her. She pulled her head away from his to meet his gaze and laugh softly. "The great base ballist, Dexter Riley, afraid?"

"Terrified. You, Miss Chambers, are far more frightening than any flying ball or tossed willow."

His arms encircled her, and she rested against his chest with a contentment that was new to her. His embrace was a haven, enclosing the two of them from time and reality.

"There's something I must tell ye."

Unease slipped into her peace at the cautious note in his voice and the tell-tale Irish accent. Was there some reason he shouldn't care for her? Had he promised himself to another?

"I don't usually tell people much about my past, but I want ye to know the truth about me, right from the beginning."

Truth? *Beginning*? Which word made her nerve endings tinkle like icicles in the wind?

"My grandparents hadn't much money when they arrived from Ireland during the famine, but Da's parents had a mite more than most. Enough to establish a business." She heard him swallow, felt his chest rise with a ragged breath. "A saloon."

Her heart stopped for the space of a beat, then continued on. "Your *grandfather* started this saloon?"

He nodded.

A little wave of relief trickled over her. Two generations had passed since then. It wasn't as though Dexter was a saloon keeper.

He cleared his voice and continued. "They had ten children. Da was oldest, fourteen when they came to America. Da intended to leave the saloon when he married Mother. He wanted to farm land in the northwest. But Grandfather died almost immediately after they married, and Da took over the saloon. He needed the money to raise his brothers and sisters.

"Mother always hated the saloon. She had to help in it. All of us children were brought up in it. Some of my brothers and sisters—there's six of us—are barely younger than my youngest uncle."

"Your parents were essentially raising two families."

"Yes. My older brothers and sisters helped out when they were old enough. Mother used to tell of Amanda and me crawling about underfoot in the kitchen where she could keep an eye on us. She never allowed us to work in the bar area, but we saw and heard plenty, just the same."

His fingers tightened over hers. The gas light standing sentry nearby gained a halo from the mist in her eyes. How different his childhood had been from hers, where serenity filled their modest parsonage.

"Mother was determined at least two of her children wouldna grow up to work in a saloon. She constantly reminded Amanda and me that we must get all the education possible and do something respectable with our lives.

"She made sure we went to church, too. We weren't too old before we discovered why she wanted us away from the saloon. Many parents, especially the church members, wouldna let their kids play with us.

"I like Base Ball. Most of the people in the part of the city where we grew up liked the sport. I was not knowing the wealthier classes disapproved of it. So when I had the chance to sign with the Louisville Eclipse, a minor league team, for more money than I thought a fifteen-year-old boy would ever see, I grabbed it, glad to be getting away from the saloon like Mother wanted.

"Then Da and Mother were killed in a train accident."

She touched her lips to the back of one huge hand. She hadn't known he and Amanda had lost their parents.

"My oldest brother, Frank, took over the saloon, The Irish Stars. I moved into an apartment with another base baller."

"After joining the Eclipse, did you continue your education

as your mother wished?"

"Yes. Had time in the winter, when the ball clubs dinna play. And attended night school. Slow going, but eventually I was accepted at Washington University, where I met your brother. 'Course, it's slow going there, too, since I can't take classes year 'round. Hope to be a counselor at law one day. Can't play Base Ball all my life. A man's body won't take the strain."

"Your mother would be proud of you."

His lips pressed against her temple, tipping her hat.

"I wanted ye to know, lass. If ye find it disconcerting to be escorted by a base baller whose family owns a saloon, then it would be a kindness if ye'd tell me now, before I lose my heart to ye further."

The huskiness in his voice brought out her protective instincts. "*You* don't own the saloon, and you are not a drinking man. I think you are. . .wonderful."

"Oh, Carrie, girleen. . . "

She lifted her lips eagerly to meet his kiss.

A long while later, his chest lifted beneath her cheek in a deep sigh. "I wish I could see you tomorrow, but the club is traveling to Louisville. We meet the Eclipse there again the following day."

"But you've played them three times already this week."

"We meet them five times in this series, and the last two match games will be at their ball grounds."

She did some quick calculating. This was Thursday. If the next game was Saturday. . .

She pushed away from him, trying to curb her panic. "But that means you won't be back until we've gone home."

"We'll arrive back Monday morning."

Disappointment was too swamping for her to hide. "I was hoping you would attend church with us Sunday. Father has been asked to give the sermon at the church that is considering calling him." Then it dawned on her, and she sat up straighter, unconsciously adjusting the hat which had slipped over one ear.

"If you have two match games left with Louisville, and you're returning Sunday night, you will be playing on Sunday."

"We have no choice. It's one of the tenants of the American Association league, that the clubs play on Sundays in the cities where it's legal."

She tried to search his eyes, but it was too dark to see them clearly, though she heard the wariness in his reply. "You agree to play on the Lord's Day?" she asked slowly.

"I must. All the players must. If we don't, Von der Ahe could let us go."

"Let you go?"

"Release us from our contracts."

"Couldn't you sign with a club that doesn't require you to play on Sundays?"

He gave a slight laugh that was almost a snort. "A player can't simply choose the club he'll play on, he has to be asked. And no clubs in the National League, which doesn't play on Sundays, have asked me. Besides, I want to play in St. Louis, for my hometown, and I want to play in a major league.

"Did you *know* when you agreed to play for the Browns that you would be required to play on Sundays?"

"Yes." The single syllable was crisp.

"I see."

He pulled his hat off and ran a hand distractedly through his thick hair. "It isn't easy to start a new major league. The club owners invest a lot of money. They want to be sure they draw enough spectators so they won't be losing their investment. Most ordinary laborers work six days a week. The only day they have free to attend a match is Sunday."

"But it's the Lord's Day."

They were both quiet for a long time, over five minutes by the clock in the leather reins' holder attached to the carriage's dashboard, Carrie noticed.

His hand caressed her shoulder. When he finally spoke, his voice vibrated with misery. "I can't be changing the fact that for most people Sunday is a holy day, nor can I be changing the fact that I'm obligated by my contract to play any day Der Boss orders it. But I'm not wanting to leave ye tonight with this between us."

"I don't want that either," she whispered. "We won't allow it to stand between us."

With a ragged sigh, he wrapped his arms tightly about her.

Pain twisted in the middle of her chest. He would be gone until Monday. She didn't know when she might see him again, and the uncertainty was unbearable.

"When the train gets in Monday, I'll come straight to the hotel. If ye are still in town, will ye wait for me there?"

Relief eased the pain, but the tears spilled over. She nodded, unable to speak. Unclasping her handbag, she removed a delicate lace handkerchief never meant for serious use, and dabbed at her cheeks.

With an exclamation of concern, he leaned over her, one hand closing over hers with the handkerchief. "You're crying!"

Pride abandoned her. "I shall miss you." He couldn't have heard the wobbly words if his face wasn't so near hers.

He crushed her to himself, and she thought in embarrassment that his cheek would be wet from her tears. "I'll think of you every moment we're apart. I'll not be worth anything to Der Boss in Louisville!"

A church bell rang the midnight hour, and she could feel the reluctance with which he pulled away. "I'd best be for getting you back, or your father will be having me hide, and properly so."

But before he took the reins again, he gently pulled her hand through his arm, and her shoulder rested intimately against his until they reached the hotel. She felt a desperate need to cherish every moment granted her with this man who had such a hold on her heart.

❧

Dexter couldn't wait to get back to St. Louis—to Carrie, he

corrected himself—and they'd barely left the St. Louis depot.

He'd wanted to tell her last night that he was in love with her, but how could he expect her to believe it on such short acquaintance? Still, it seemed ungentlemanly to ask for and accept her embrace without declaring his intentions. Her kisses were innocent and sweet. The eagerness with which she'd welcomed his arms humbled him, for he knew it meant she cared. She wasn't the type of woman who gave her kisses lightly, expecting no promises.

Not that he'd ever exchanged more than a couple kisses with any woman. He wanted more that an evening with a woman. He wanted a lifetime—with the *right* woman.

With Carrie.

Would she be willing to share life with a base baller?

He'd thought Base Ball would release him from the reputation of being raised in a saloon. He'd been wrong. Base Ball wasn't respected by his "social betters." They liked meeting base ballers and watching them play, but didn't consider them equals. More like toys or baubles to dangle in front of their friends. Some of the base ballers, maybe most of them, responded by using the people who tried to use them. Fair exchange, the players thought. They only hurt themselves and the silly hangers-on. Couldn't see beyond the moment.

That was why it was so important he continue with his law courses. One day he'd be a counselor, a man whose profession wouldn't shame Carrie. If she'd have him.

The thought of losing her twisted his stomach with an unfamiliar fear.

five

Carrie stared out between the hotel room's velvet window dressings into the busy street below. The incessant clang-clang of rushing cable cars in the next thoroughfare appeared to set the pace for pedestrians and horse-drawn vehicles. Eight o'clock, and the city was already bustling with businessmen rushing to their day.

She'd seen hundreds—it seemed like thousands to someone with her small-town background—of workers dashing along the city's streets during the past week. Bankers, lawyers, architects, office-boys, draymen, hackmen: vocation and age were of no matter, they all presented the same demeanor. They scurried about at an impatient clip, each trying to exceed the speed of the person ahead. Tension shouted from the set of their shoulders, whether below finely hand-tailored suits or poorly fitting jackets purchased from a cheap emporium. Strain-chiseled furrows marked their faces.

They were so unlike Dexter at his work, or away from it for that matter. Some of his clubmates scowled while they played, heaped abuses on members of the opposing club, and even resorted to kicking and fisticuffs, but not Dexter. Beneath his mustache, his smile never left his face, only changed in degree. Tiny lines rayed from his wide-set eyes despite his youth, but the lines were a badge earned squinting against the summer suns during years of Base Ball, not carved from business worries.

She was glad he was content in his vocation, though his choice of profession did cause her a niggling worry. She preferred he not work on the Lord's Day, and in an atmosphere which did not include spectators drinking beer and other spirits.

At least Dexter wasn't a drinking man, she thought with relief. Of course, she wouldn't have been attracted to him if he were one. She had never allowed a drinking man to escort her. What was the sense of becoming involved with a man who had habits she knew she would not want in a husband?

Husband. She'd always thought Emmet would be her husband. Now she knew that in spite of her fondness for him, something was missing.

Dear Emmet, who had been her close friend through the years, then her first escort, and who waited patiently and trustingly for the day they would marry. They didn't share great passion—even the word heated her cheeks, remembering the way she responded to Dexter. But she and Emmet had an honest enjoyment of each other's company, a respect for each other's ideals, and a shared joy in their faith in Christ. With his quiet, almost gentle nature, and plain face beneath straight, dishwater blonde hair, he would never compare well to a man like Dexter Riley, at least in most women's minds. But she knew Emmet was finer than most men. She'd known when he was a boy that he'd grow up to the that kind of man: one who would always do the honorable thing, with no fanfare and no excuses and no hesitation. The kind of man who would gain the respect and trust of men, women, and children.

After all these years, and all the warm moments and special dreams they'd shared, she couldn't bring his face clearly to mind. The only face she could picture was Dexter Riley's, with its confident, laughing green eyes beneath straight, thick brows, and the mustache that covered his top lip, framing his smiling mouth. Her heart had never quivered uncomfortably at Emmet's smile, though it did at Dexter's.

It was unthinkable to be attracted to a man on such short acquaintance, and a base ballist at that! Shame fought with the attraction in her breast. How could she for a moment be interested in him when she had the love of a man like Emmet?

Well, doubtless the attraction would pass. Dexter would tire of her, and in a few weeks, she would forget she was reacting so foolishly.

Arms crossed over her tailored promenade polonaise of

sapphire blue, she leaned her forehead lightly against the window glass and rubbed her upper arms in their narrow sleeves. The city had lost its glow of excitement for her since Dexter left for Louisville. It wasn't that the past three days had been unpleasant, but that she had merely been but passing time until Dexter returned.

Now Monday morning had arrived, and her parents had the day planned for them: the last day before they returned to their home town to await the decision of the local congregation. She glanced at the marcasite-set watch pinned to her polonaise; *ten past eight*. With a sigh, she picked up the ivory-vellum envelope containing the note she'd written telling Dexter where she'd be for the day. She retrieved the bonnet that matched her promenade outfit and, swinging it carelessly by its satin tics, went down to the lobby to await her parents.

She had just left the note at the desk when she felt a touch on her arm and heard her name spoken by the voice that had already grown dear to her. Joy washed everything else from her senses.

She whirled to face him and he captured her hands in his own, his eyes roaming over her face as though he was starved for the sight of her. His obvious pleasure in once again being in her company filled her with wonder.

"I didn't think you would. . . " she started.

"I was afraid I wouldn't. . . " he began at the same time.

They laughed together at their stumbling start.

"I was afraid you would be gone," he said, and the thankfulness in his tone spread warmth through her. "I came directly from the depot."

"We leave tomorrow morning. Grant is showing us Washington University today. He's eager for us to become familiar with his school."

He rubbed the palm of one knotty-knuckled hand over his face and grinned. "I need to freshen up, and shave again. I tried to shave on the train, but I'm afraid I wasn't too successful." Half-a-dozen brown-red nicks along his chin and neck attested to the fact. "Do you think your parents might allow me to steal you away this afternoon? I could show you Lafayette Park in daylight."

It was on the tip of her tongue to say that the afternoon was much too far in the future, but she caught back the unladylike statement and nodded eagerly.

It was a lovely afternoon for rowing, Carrie thought later, leaning back against the cushions Dexter had thoughtfully provided. The day was warm for early May, so the breeze off the water wasn't chilling. A canvas top over the swan-shaped boat protected them from the sun's rays. She trailed the fingers of one hand in the barely-ruffled waters and watched Dexter row.

"What are you thinking?"

She cast him a frankly flirtatious grin. "That you remind me of a Venetian gondolier."

He rolled his eyes and shook his head. "Faith, and I've given my heart to a romantic!"

Her breath caught in her chest at his words. Had he truly given her his heart, or was he simply speaking the blarney that falls easily from the lips of a man who is sought after by women? For the moment, at least, she resolved to believe it. She didn't want anything to mar these last hours with him before leaving the city.

He rested his chest against the hands gripping the oars. "Happy?"

"Oh, yes! It's perfect."

"The lake, or the company?"

"Both are perfect. Everything is perfect. Or. . . "

"Or?"

"It would be perfect, if you didn't have to play Sunday ball."

He bent to the oars once more, their dipping motion making a pleasant "plash." "Nothing has changed since we last discussed this. I don't know what else I can say."

She leaned forward earnestly, her elbows on the knees which were draped by her tailored, sapphire-blue skirt. "But if you told Mr. Von der Ahe it was against your religious beliefs to work on Sunday, surely he would release you from the need to do so."

Frowning, he looked away quickly, then back to her. "More likely he would release me from the need to play on any day."

She looked out over the water. She shouldn't have broached the topic. It only added a depressing note to the otherwise lovely afternoon.

"Besides—" he started, then he broke off.

She turned back to him when he didn't continue.

Looking directly into her eyes, he spoke gently. "Besides, it isn't against my religious beliefs to play on Sundays."

She tilted her head, frowning. "Surely the church you attend teaches the third commandment, 'Remember the Sabbath Day, to keep it holy.'"

"I don't attend church."

Her blood turned to ice. He *couldn't* be an unbeliever, he couldn't, her mind argued. She could never have fallen in love with a man who didn't love the Lord. "Why?" The one word croaked from her tight throat.

"When Mother was alive, I attended regularly. Church was important to her, so I and the rest of the family went every Sunday. But we went to please her, not because it was important to us. Only me Da never went. He didn't believe in God, and said on the chance he was mistaken about His existence, he wasn't about to dishonor Him by pretending to worship Him when he didn't believe."

Her chest trembled at his words. "You. . .don't believe in God?"

"I don't believe in Him or not believe in Him. If He exists, He doesn't appear to pay attention to the people He made, so I can't be seeing that it will disturb Him if I'm not paying Him much mind."

"How can you say God doesn't take notice of us, when He sent His own Son to take the punishment for our sins?"

"I know Jesus walked this earth, but I don't know that He was the Son of God. How can I believe Jesus is God's Son, when I don't even know whether I believe God exists?"

She had no answer to that. "Does Amanda believe?"

"She feels as I do."

Carrie looked across the water, wondering that it could be so calm when she felt she was in the midst of a hurricane. Five minutes ago her world was almost perfect, and now—now everything wonderful had been ripped from her.

Nothing was what it seemed. She'd always thought believers were Good People, in spite of their imperfections, and that unbelievers were Bad People, with imperfections impossible to miss. But Amanda wasn't a horrible person, and Dexter. . . Her gaze slid back to him, and she studied the handsome, pleasant face, now without its usual charming smile. Dexter certainly wasn't an awful person. It was all so confusing.

The Bible's command wasn't confusing, however. It clearly warned that believers and unbelievers weren't to wed. How could a person who loved God be truly one with a person who did not believe in Him, let alone love Him and choose to follow His ways?

Over the last few days, she had started pushing Emmet from thoughts of her future, and replaced him with the dream of a life with Dexter. The dream would have to die, and the knowledge tore through her, leaving a gaping wound in place of her heart.

She was quiet during the few minutes it took to land the boat and return it to the docksman, responding only with a nod or a single word when Dexter addressed her.

Dexter drew her from the public shoreline to a bench, obscured by a large clump of lilac bushes, their buds flooding the air with their distinctive, cloying scent.

When they were seated, Dexter rested a rough palm against her cheek with a gentleness that made her ache anew. "I can't be bearing to think of your leaving tomorrow, girleen. I'd follow, but I can't. I can't even be promising to visit ye in your home town often. We have ninety-six matches scheduled this season, and will be traveling all over the central and eastern states to play in addition to the matches we play here and the exhibition matches. I'm not wanting to be apart from ye. I know this is sudden, Carrie, but—I'm loving ye so! Will ye marry me, as soon as possible?"

Marry him! Such a short time ago it would have been the sweetest request in the world. Now she recognized the cruelty in it.

"I can't. I can't marry you."

six

"Why won't ye marry me, Carrie? Because of that Emmet Wilson? Ye can't be loving him. Ye love *me.* Surely ye can't be denying it."

"No." Carrie rested an unsteady hand on his crisp linen shirt front. "No, I can't deny it." The words were barely a whisper. She wondered that he even heard them, but he must have, because his strong, huge arms surrounded her, hauling her against his chest until she could smell the fresh-ironed scent of his shirt mixed with the popular scent of bay rum cologne.

"Tell me, Carrie. Tell me ye love me."

His Irish accent was urgent against her hair. She could feel his need to hear her declaration in the stiffness of his limbs, in the way his broad chest stilled with his baited breath.

She couldn't possibly marry him when he didn't love the Lord. She'd never allow herself to see him again after today. But her heart and mind had been battering to speak her love of him for days. Perhaps it was unwise, but she wanted to say the words to him. *Just today, and never again, forever.*

Her arms crept around his neck. She tightened her hold on him, leaned her cheek against his own recently shaved one, and whispered the words she'd waited a lifetime to say. "I love you. I love you, Dexter!"

His breath whooshed out in relief. He stood, pulling her with him, and nearly squeezed the breath out of her in the next instant when he lifted her off her feet with his hug. "I knew it!"

She laughed through the tears in her throat. Her hands pushed ineffectually against his shoulders. "Put me down. What if someone should see us?"

"I'll not put you down until you promise to marry me."

Her laughter stilled into a small, closed smile, and she averted her gaze from his.

His arms froze once more, and she wished she never had to hear him ask the words she knew were coming. If only time could stop at this moment, could stay filled always with his first joyous knowledge of their shared love.

"Say ye'll marry me, Carrie." His voice was tight, urgent, wary.

She couldn't bear to look at him, so hugged him closer, his hair against her cheek.

He lowered her slowly until her feet touched the ground. "Look at me."

She knew her eyes were filled with sadness, that he'd see it and know her answer to his proposal, but she met his gaze. The pain there crashed through her, washing over her with the ferocity of a tidal wave.

"If ye love me, why be ye hurting us both this way?

His voice was thick with torment. It filled her with aching regret. She shouldn't have let it go this far. She should have done as her conscience demanded, stayed faithful to Emmet and refused to see Dexter apart from the family. Instead she'd told herself she couldn't possibly lose her heart to him.

She swallowed, her throat almost closed from pain. "We don't share a faith in the Lord. We can't marry without that."

He stared at her stupidly. "Ye aren't refusing me to marry another man, but refusing me because I'm not knowing what I believe about God?"

"I decided years ago that the Lord was the most important thing—Person—in my life, and I promised Him I would always put Him first."

"But I dinna object to your attending church. I'm not objecting to your faith. I wouldn't be asking ye to forsake it."

"I know, but the Bible says believers aren't to marry unbelievers."

He stepped back from her, looking as if he'd been slapped, and she was suddenly cold, standing there without his arms about her. His face was colder, chilling her through with its anger and hurt.

She reached for him impulsively, longing to draw him back into her embrace, to comfort him and make him understand that she wanted nothing more in the world than to be his wife, but the choice wasn't hers.

He stepped back, just beyond her reach. She felt stranded, as if she were on an island near a populated shoreline with no rescue in sight.

His jaw tightened. She knew he was struggling to keep his temper at bay. "I won't pretend that I'll change for ye. I won't be a hypocrite and pretend to serve a God I'm not certain exists."

"I don't wish you to become a hypocrite." She took a step toward him, eager to get closer, where it would be easier to talk.

He stepped back again, bringing himself abruptly against the trunk of a huge elm.

She could take advantage of that elm, she thought, but what was the point when he so obviously did not want her touch?

"I can't be promising to become a believer, either, or even that I will try to become one."

She nodded. Of course he couldn't promise to become a believer. How could anyone promise such a thing?

They stared at each other. Was misery as heavy in her face as it was in his? The minutes grew long, and the air filled with the sounds of others enjoying the lake beyond the screen of fragrant lilac bushes, oblivious to two lives that would never be the same after this afternoon.

"I love ye. Ye say ye love me. That's all that's important. Don't let this silly thing keep us apart." His voice was husky with pain. He reached for her.

But this time it was she who retreated. If she allowed herself to be held in those arms for even a moment more, she just might forget that "silly thing," and turn her back on her Lord—who never turned His back on her—and stay forever in Dexter's embrace.

She shook her head slightly. "I love you, but I can't marry you."

She stumbled slightly over an unexpected rise in the path, caught herself, turned and fled.

❧

One can't flee the pain of spending life without the one you love, she thought four months later, staring out the parlor window at her mother's garden in back of the St. Louis parsonage.

If only her father hadn't accepted the call to the St. Louis church! Now she couldn't leave the house without watching for Dexter, hoping their paths would cross, knowing they mustn't or her heart would play her traitor.

The days on which match games were played at Sportsman's Park were the worst. She forced herself to stay away, but couldn't concentrate on work or conversations. Knowing where he was, knowing it was within her power to see him, made it impossible to think of anything else.

It didn't help that the citizens were so taken with the St. Louis Browns. The twenty-five-cent entrance fee, serving of beer at the ball grounds, and Sunday match games garnered a loyal following for the American Association—or the "Beer and Whiskey League" as it was so appropriately and popularly called.

She heard the names of the clubs and members spoken often by boys and men who followed the sport as though their livelihoods depended upon the scores. The best players' names were becoming as well known as the names of politicians, especially the local players. Mullane and Browning were often mentioned as rising stars, and she couldn't hear their names without remembering Dexter and their first evening together at the bridge.

Dexter wasn't gaining the fame of his two friends, but he had garnered quite a following just the same. He was, as he had said, considered a consistently good player, though not one of the sports' shining stars, good both at hitting and in the outfield, which apparently could not be said for most players. His reputation was that of a player who would not drink, or fight, or play unfairly.

He hadn't played unfairly with her, either. He hadn't pretended he would serve God when he learned she would not marry a man who was not committed to the Lord. She was the one who had been unfair; unfair to herself, and Dexter, and Emmet. She'd had no right to spend time with Dexter when she'd allowed Emmet to think she would marry him.

Her attention was caught by the red roses swaying in the gentle breeze. Most of the pink and red flowers which had dotted the garden when the family moved in two months ago were being replaced by cheerful yellow, orange, and russet blooms.

She wished she could believe her heart would also be cheerful soon. She'd believed it at first. Believed she would be able to forget Dexter. Believed one morning she'd wake up and no longer hurt when she remembered he was gone from her life forever. Believed she'd see a child without wondering what it would have been like to raise a family with Dexter, wondering what his children would look like, imagining him grin watching them play. Believed one day she would smile without pretense, happy with life.

Believed she'd truly come to love Emmet Wilson as deeply as she loved Dexter. After all, Emmet was everything she wanted in a man. He was a Christian, moral, intelligent, and kind. He would make a good husband and father. They'd share the joy of serving the Lord, and raise their children to love Him.

Except she couldn't marry Emmet. It wasn't right to marry someone as good as Emmet with a heart that was filled with another. Emmet deserved a better love and marriage than that. She'd shied away from telling him so for a week now. He would be calling Saturday; she'd tell him then.

The thumping of brass against brass sounded dully from the hallway, and a moment later she heard her mother's steps hurry toward the door. Her mother hadn't mentioned guests were expected today, she thought idly.

Filled with an overwhelming weariness, she leaned her forehead against the cool pane. Disgust at herself for the manner in which she was treating Emmet engulfed her. She'd always despised women who treated a man's love like a worthless toy, discardable when it no longer suited. Now she was treating Emmet's love in that despicable way.

"Lord, if it is the only thing I learn in life, teach me to love as Thou dost love," she whispered.

"You have a visitor, Carrie."

At her mother's soft voice, she turned from the window, startled. Her heart zoomed to the floor faster than one of the fancy wrought-iron elevators in the Palace Hotel where she'd dined with Dexter, for there he stood, his gaze anxiously searching her face over her mother's head.

Mrs. Chambers looked uncertainly from one to the other, tightened her thin lips, and quietly left the room.

Carrie loosened her grip on the rich tapestry drapery. She hadn't realized she'd crushed the fabric in her fist when she saw Dexter in the doorway. She should stop staring at him, greet him, welcome him into the parlor in proper manner, but she couldn't gather her wits. He looked so good, standing in the doorway in his gray suit, his matching bowler in one hand at his side, his wine-red hair slightly mussed from pulling off his hat.

He slid one hand into his trouser pocket, letting his weight rest mostly on one leg. His eyes looked quickly off to one side, then returned to her before he raised his eyebrows and quirked one corner of his mouth into a smile. The gesture was over in a moment, but its sweet familiarity sent a cool, jelly-like curl through her stomach. He was as frightened and uncomfortable as herself, and as glad to see her as she was to see him.

"Hello, Carrie." In spite of his smile, his eyes were bright with uncertainty.

She started to grip the drapery again, caught herself just in time and clutched her hands behind her. "Hello, Dexter."

He shrugged his shoulders and eyebrows at the same time. "May I come in?"

"I. . .I'm not certain that would be wise."

"Don't ask me to leave. Please."

The huskiness in his plea made the muscles in her legs melt. She reached behind her, gripping the window sash through the filmy lace undercurtain with both hands to steady herself.

The mustache above his smile was trembling just like her legs, she realized, astonished. Her gaze darted to his eyes, and the pain standing there stark and bare seared her.

"Why—" The word came out of her dry throat like a croak. She swallowed and tried again. "Why are you here?"

He shifted his weight, one hand remaining in his pocket, the other rhythmically bouncing the bowler off his thigh. "I hoped ye might reconsider."

"Reconsider?"

His gaze darted away and back again. "Reconsider marrying me."

Hope set her heart soaring. "You've changed your mind? You believe in the Lord?"

His lips pressed together until the furrows bracketing them whitened. "No."

Disappointment chased away the hope in her chest. "Then—"

He crossed the room swiftly, his steps thudding dully in the thick Brussels carpet. He tossed the bowler to one side, not watching whether it landed on the round table he passed.

He stopped directly in front of her, so close she would bump his chest if she swayed ever so slightly. His gaze burned into hers, longing mingled with pain. "I was not knowing it was possible for a man to hurt as much as I've been hurting over ye." He gave her his silly, crooked grin. It didn't erase the glaze in his eyes. The knowledge only hurt her more. "Hurt more than the time a hurler hit me arm with the ball when I was batsman. Broke it. The arm, not the bat." The grin slipped slowly away. "Don't be turning me away again, girleen."

His low-spoken words trembled in the small space between them. He opened his arms slowly, but didn't move to take her into them. She realized he was waiting for her to choose. The fresh smell of soap and manly cologne and starched shirt wrapped around her. Her gaze caught tight in his.

She swayed slightly toward him. In a moment his arms were around her, her cheek pressed against the weave of his linen jacket. She'd fought the desire to be in his embrace for months, and his arms felt incredibly good.

One of his hands slid to the back of her neck. "I love you, Carrie!"

Tears burned her eyes, and she pressed her cheek tighter against his chest. How was she going to make herself walk away from him again? Last time had been difficult enough. Now that she'd allowed him to hold her. . .now that she'd allowed herself to be held, she corrected silently, how was she going to walk away from this man who made her feel more wonderful than anyone else?

She took a shaky breath. "I love you, too, but, the Lord. . . "

His arms tightened. Was he afraid she would push herself away from him?

"My beliefs haven't changed. I'd do most anything to please ye, but not lie to God, or about believing in Him. But I'll go to church with ye, and I'll never stop ye from doing what ye think is right."

If he goes to church, surely Thou canst speak to him, Lord. If I don't marry him, he might continue to stay away from church, and Thou might never reach him. Am I to be Thy way of bringing him to Thee? A sliver of unease slipped through her at her argument. It didn't stand up well against the Bible's admonition to believers not to marry unbelievers.

His hands closed lightly but firmly about her shoulders, and he pushed her slightly away until their gazes could meet. She smiled and touched his cheek with trembling fingertips. "In my heart, I am already your wife, my love."

Joy followed unbelief in his eyes. The grin she loved spread wide beneath the red-tinged mustache. She longed for him to kiss her, but he glanced away again, then back. "Is it certain ye are?"

She nodded eagerly.

One arm held her close, the rough, blunt fingertips of the other tracing her cheek with a gentleness that awed her. "I can hardly be waiting to marry ye, girleen." The words were a whisper against her lips, and she thanked him with a kiss.

Doubt rumbled like distant thunder in her mind and chest, but she pushed it away, rejoicing in the wonder and beauty of Dexter's love.

seven

"You're going to marry that. . .that. . .*base ballist*?" Reverend Chambers bolted from the cavernous comfort of the upholstered chair in his study, his black coat trembling on his sparse frame. Thin black brows broken with a spattering of gray hairs arched above the eyes so like Carrie's, eyes which glowered at her, almost shaking her determination.

Lifting her chin, Carrie attempted to return his gaze evenly. She must make him see there was no chance he could sway her; he mustn't suspect the way she quailed inside at his displeasure. She forced her lips into a smile, hoping her father wouldn't notice their propensity to quiver. "Yes, aren't you fortunate? Think how popular you'll be with the men in the congregation as the father-in-law of one of the country's best base ballists."

The expression on his narrow face was anything but pleased. "Players of Base Ball are hardly considered men of high moral or *spiritual* character."

Carrie moved to the mantle, forcing a bounce into her step, and unnecessarily rearranged the silver candle holders to keep from facing him for a moment. "Isn't it wonderful Dexter is the exception?"

His snort of disgust would have done a horse justice.

Carrie squeezed her eyes tightly together. This discussion was going worse than she'd anticipated. With a quick prayer, she turned about to face him again, her fingers linked loosely behind her. She kept her voice light with an effort. "You can't deceive me, Father. I know you like Dexter. I've heard you tell Grant what a fine man he is."

"Not fine enough to marry my daughter." Anger increased the craggy effect of his features, making him look cruel, belying the kind nature she knew lay in his heart.

She tipped the corners of her lips with the teasing smile she'd used to win her way from him innumerable times in the past. "You would think that of any man I wished to marry."

His glower didn't weaken. "What about Emmet Wilson?"

Her gaze dropped to the floor. *Emmet.* She hated the way this would hurt him. She hated the shame and disgrace that wormed its way through her chest whenever her conscience reminded her of her disloyalty to him. Still, even if she didn't marry Dexter, she couldn't marry Emmet. Not now.

She swallowed the painful lump in her throat that had traitorously absorbed her voice. "Would it be a kindness to marry Emmet when I lo. . .when I love Dexter?" Silly how difficult it was to express her love for a man to her father.

His frown deepened, the thin brows meeting above the long, narrow nose. The anger in his eyes faded into confusion and sorrow while his gaze searched her face. He rested slender hands on her shoulders. "There can be no lasting happiness for you with a man who doesn't share your love for God."

His voice was rough with concern for her, and she fought against its effect. "Until Dexter, I never thought it possible I could love a man who didn't share my beliefs. Now, I can't imagine spending the rest of my life without him."

The hands slipped from her shoulders, and he wiped them over his face as though attempting to wipe the last few minutes from existence. "God hasn't given us laws and commandments only to show us how imperfect we are, but as guides to a life of joy, peace, and contentment. He warns us not to marry those who don't share our faith because He knows the sorrows that lie along that path. How can there be joy ahead for you if you try to follow God, and Dexter is following his own desires? How can you be one?"

"I tried refusing him, Father. When Dexter asked me to marry him last May, I insisted I couldn't because he doesn't trust in Christ. I told him I was going to marry Emmet. I thought if I tried to do as God wished, He would remove my love for Dexter and increase my love for Emmet. But He didn't. I've hurt every waking moment since walking away from Dexter last May, until he returned yesterday, and asked me again to be his wife."

His lips thinned into a determined line. "You'll know greater pain if you marry him."

Slowly she reached for his hands. He allowed her to hold them without returning the pressure of her fingers. "You've always told me God can do anything. Did you mean He can do anything but change Dexter's heart, anything but make Dexter a believer?"

"You know God allows each person to decide for himself whether to love and follow Him."

She started to argue, but he cut in quickly.

"If a man is drowning, it is easier for the drowning man to pull his would-be rescuer down with him than it is for the would-be rescuer to save the drowning man. It is the same when we share our lives with those who don't follow God. It is easier to be enticed from the Lord's way than to convince another to follow Him."

She dropped his hands, took a deep breath, and threw her shoulders back. "I don't intend to allow Dexter to drown, whatever the risk to me. I'd hoped for your blessing, but I expect you will not allow yourself to give it."

Sadness carved itself deeply into his face, buried itself in the caverns of his eyes. "I cannot."

Her chest burned with frustration, fury, despair. "I shall marry Dexter without your blessing, then. I shall love him into God's kingdom myself, if I must. But I'll not spend the rest of my days without him."

❧

Her father wasn't nearly as formidable to face as Emmet.

Carrie hadn't seen much of him since her family moved to St. Louis. He'd spent the summer in Ridgeville, their home town, working in his father's store. They'd corresponded regularly, however, and Emmet had occasionally visited.

He'd arrived in St. Louis this afternoon, and would be staying with Carrie's family and leaving on the train Monday morning for his last year at the University. He and Carrie had planned this evening for a long time: dinner at the magnificent Lindell Hotel. Emmet had suggested the Planter's,where she had eaten with Dexter, but Carrie couldn't bear the thought of the memories it would raise. Not that she told Emmet her reason for wishing to eat elsewhere, of course. And easy-going Emmet never suspected a thing.

She found the evening most trying. If she told him of Dexter at the beginning of the evening, the entire night would be ruined for him. But she could think of nothing but the truth she must eventually reveal, and she was unaccustomedly quiet.

The parsonage was a lovely home, built of stone, with a wide porch along the front and sides. A number of cushion-filled wicker chairs were scattered about the porch, with a large wicker swing at one end of the front portion. It was to the swing Emmet led her when they arrived back from dinner.

Light from the silk-shaded parlor lamp shone mellow through the huge window, which was topped with colorful leaded glass. There was enough light for her to see his face clearly in spite of the late hour. A few houses down the street, a family was on their own porch, enjoying the mild evening, singing softly to the accompaniment of a guitar.

Emmet kept her hand in his when they sat down in the swing.

He shifted to face her, pushed the swing into rhythmic movement with his foot, and briefly touched his lips to her gloved fingers. His eyes smiled at her over their joined hands. "The music makes a nice background for a man to say good-bye to his favorite girl."

She noted his narrow lips, so different from Dexter's. Emmet had kissed her numerous times through the years, but never with the passion in Dexter's kisses. Of course, one couldn't marry a man because of the way he kissed!

She tucked her chin against the lacy breast of her dress, avoiding his gaze. "I. . .there's something I must tell you."

"Must be pretty serious. The last time you avoided looking at me, you told me you'd freed my pet frog."

The memory brought a welcome, releasing laugh, and she met his gaze with merry accusation. "Frogs aren't meant to live in boxes, even to keep ten-year-old boys happy."

He shook his head. "Ten years old. Seems like we've known each other forever."

The laughter died. She looked sharply away. "Yes."

She suddenly realized that she would miss his comfortable company. There would be no more evenings of talking and laughing together. No more discussions of the Bible, or friendly arguments over the meaning of certain passages. No more times of prayer together for each other's needs, or those of friends or family. She had been acutely aware that her marriage to Dexter would hurt Emmet; she hadn't realized until this moment that she would miss him, the same as she would miss Grant if he disappeared suddenly from her world.

His soft, tapered fingers touched her cheek, urging her to face him. "Darling, what's wrong?"

She looked into the face as familiar to her as her own and batted away the tears in her eyes. "I don't want to hurt you." The words were barely a whisper.

His eyebrows met in a puzzled frown, and his hand slipped from her cheek.

She took a deep breath, wringing the dainty handkerchief in her lap with both hands. "Do you remember Dexter Riley?"

He nodded. "Of course. Grant's friend, the one who plays on the St. Louis Browns."

"I. . .I've promised to marry him."

The music down the street filled the silence. The ache in her chest and throat grew to mammoth proportions. Wouldn't he ever respond?

Finally he rubbed a free hand over his chin. "When you give a man news, it's a headliner."

"I'm sorry." Never had an apology seemed less adequate.

"What about us? What of all the times we talked about our plans for the future?"

"You. . .never actually *asked* me to marry you."

"I presumed from the way we talked, the way we kept company, that you knew my intentions and wanted the same thing."

She stared at her hands, miserable in her guilt. She had wanted the same thing until she met Dexter. Emmet likely wouldn't find the knowledge comforting.

He took a deep breath. "I don't suppose it would do any good to ask you to marry me now?"

She caught her bottom lip between her teeth and shook

her head.

"I was afraid of that." He leaned back, studying her face as though he'd never seen her before. . .or was he memorizing it from fear of never seeing her again? Guilt squirmed through her at the confusion in his amber eyes.

"I wish there were a way I could marry Dexter without hurting you."

His narrow lips twisted in the first sarcastic smile she'd seen on his face since he was fourteen. "It doesn't work that way, darl. . .it doesn't work that way."

The music stopped. Voices drifted down to them. A door squeaked open and slammed shut. Then only the swing's creak filled the awful chasm between them.

Her chest felt as though it must burst. If she hurt this bad, what must Emmet be experiencing?

"I can't imagine not having you in my life, Carrie."

"I feel the same."

A wry, harsh laugh broke from his lips and tore through her. "I doubt you feel *exactly* the same."

The swing continued its back and forth journey, going nowhere. But their lives had changed course, Carrie thought.

"This Riley, is he a Christian?"

She shook her head, not daring to meet his gaze.

The swing stopped.

"Surely you aren't going to marry a man who doesn't follow the Lord?"

"I love him. I believe God will use me to show him the truth."

He grabbed her shoulders, turning her to face him. "You know you can't count on that."

"I must."

"Don't do this. Don't marry me if you don't wish to, but don't marry a man who doesn't share your faith."

The desperation in his voice touched her more than anything had all evening. In spite of his own pain, he was concerned for her happiness. "It will work out, I promise you."

He picked up his wide-brimmed bowler from the seat beside him. "That's something you *can't* promise, and you know it."

eight

1884

Carrie slipped out of bed and opened the pale blue velvet draperies to allow July's morning sunshine to spill into the room through the lace undercurtain.

Dexter groaned and squeezed his closed eyes tighter to shut out all trace of day.

She grinned down at him, trailing the deep lace ruffle at her wrist lightly along his cheek. He tried to dodge it, his eyes still closed, then brushed feebly at it. Finally he opened his eyes, staring at her with an unfocused gaze.

"Good morning, sleepyhead."

A slow smile spread over his face. "You even look good in the morning, Mrs. Riley."

"Irish blarney! You can't even see yet; your eyes are still glazed over with sleep!" But his flattery made her feel special, just the same, she admitted to herself. She could hardly believe they'd been married almost two years!

"That's not sleep, me love. It's your beauty blinding me."

She laughed softly and stood. "More of your blarney; but I like it."

He grasped her hand. "Where are you going?"

"To dress, start breakfast, then wake our son and dress him for church."

He pulled her back down beside him, running his hands over her night robe's torchon lace sleeves. "Couldn't all that wait awhile?"

She allowed him one sweet, lazy kiss before pulling away. "If it wait, we'll be late to church. Nine-month-old boys don't dress themselves, you know. Now don't you dare go back to sleep. You need to prepare for church, too."

She was almost at the door before he said, "I don't think I'll be going to church today."

Dismay swept through her. She turned to look at him, not speaking.

"I'm tired, Carrie. Train didn't get in until four this morning. Couldn't sleep a lick on it last night, with the wheels clacking and the box rocking. The clubmates were noisy, too, celebrating yesterday's win. And we have to play this afternoon."

She wanted to beg him to come, but she knew what he said was true. He'd be too exhausted for today's match if he didn't get more sleep. Besides, when the Browns were in town, he'd been true to his promise to attend church with her since they married. Missing services this one time wouldn't change anything.

"All right, dear." She tried to swallow her disappointment, but couldn't.

❧

Two hours later Carrie and Benjamin slipped into the pew beside her mother and Grant. She smiled and whispered hellos to them, uncomfortably aware of Dexter's absence. She knew her family and others in the congregation were accustomed to seeing her and Benjamin attend services without Dexter when the St. Louis Browns had matches out of town. But she knew, too, that people were aware of the club's schedule, and knew he was playing in town today. It left her feeling vulnerable.

The plain, plumpish, gray-haired woman across the aisle gave her a pleasant nod in greeting, and Carrie returned it self-consciously. She'd always pitied devoted Mrs. Hannah Kratz, who attended every service alone. She couldn't recall ever seeing Hannah's husband attend, and her children seldom accompanied her now that they were grown.

After the service, she explained quickly to her parents and Grant why Dexter wasn't with her. She smiled and tried to act nonchalant, as though it were perfectly reasonable that he'd stayed away, and it didn't bother her a whit.

She almost convinced herself, until Hannah stopped to greet her. Sweet Hannah, with her soft smile and gentle manner, only increased Carrie's discomfort today.

The older woman rested a wrinkled, worn hand on the soft yellow silk covering Carrie's forearm. "Good morning, Mrs. Riley. How is that handsome husband of yours?"

Carrie forced a smile. "Fine, Mrs. Kratz. He didn't arrive in town until early this morning, and he needed sleep before playing this afternoon." Why had she felt compelled to offer an excuse for him?

Tiny Hannah nodded and patted Carrie's arm. *I wish she'd stop smiling that sugary sweet smile*, Carrie thought, irritated. Guilt immediately flooded her.

"I'll be praying for him. One of these days the Lord will get hold of him, you'll see."

Carrie adjusted Benjy in her arms so Hannah had to remove her hand. "Dexter will be back in church in two weeks," she assured the diminutive, wrinkled woman.

Hannah only nodded and kept smiling. "Come see me some time, my dear. We church widows must stick together."

Carrie couldn't control the shiver of distaste that ran through her. "Church widows" was the congregation's term for the women whose husbands didn't often accompany them to services. *To think when I was single I pitied such women. I never thought I'd be among them. Of course,* she hastened to reassure herself, *I'm not truly one of them. Dexter attends when possible.*

At least, he attended in body. He didn't believe in God yet, but that would come eventually.

She tried to ignore the fear that wriggled through her. The other "church widows" were younger than Hannah; their attendance without their husbands wasn't as disturbing. Like Dexter, the men likely had many years ahead of them to come to the Lord.

But Mr. Kratz was in his late sixties. Carrie didn't like to think about how long Hannah had been praying for his salvation.

Benjy stirred impatiently in her arms, and she gave him her attention, relieved to have her thoughts drawn in a more pleasant direction.

But a minute later Hannah was at her side once more. "I almost forgot, dear. A group of us are beginning a quilt for the missionary. We hoped you'd join us. We'll be meeting Tuesday evenings at my home. You're welcome to bring your son."

Why not? With Dexter out of town so often, the evenings were lonely, even with Benjy for company. "I'll be glad to join you."

Maybe if she became more involved in church projects, Dexter would realize the importance of church, she thought, watching Hannah hurry down the aisle with her bouncy waddle. She already spent Wednesday evenings at choir practice, Thursday afternoons at the women's Bible study, and she taught the children's Sunday school. But evidently that wasn't enough, because Dexter hadn't seen yet how wonderful it was to be involved in the church.

Maybe this fall, when Base Ball was over for the year, things would be different. He would be home every Sunday from November through March. Surely five months of Sundays would be enough to show him the joy of being an active church member. Dexter was not going to be another Mr. Kratz. Not if her example could change him.

❧

Dexter leaned against the door frame, one hand stuffed in a pocket of his brown flannel trousers, the other holding a cup of coffee. A warm sense of family settled inside him as he looked over the men filling their parlor: Louisville base ballers Tony Mullane and Pete Browning, and the St. Louis Browns' Charlie Comiskey, Pat Deasley, Hugh Nicol, Arlie Latham, Jumbo McGinnis, and Bob Caruthers. Except Comiskey, he was closer to these men than he was to his own brothers, and that was saying something.

He crossed his arms over his tan shirt and brown vest, chuckling at the picture they made: a group of large, rather rowdy men in casual clothes seated on his wife's dainty furniture with its curves and narrow cushions. Their chins all but rested on their knees.

Grant was the only man in the room who wasn't a base baller, and he was apparently enjoying himself just fine. That is, when he wasn't glaring at Amanda, who was flirting outrageously with Pete Browning. What was going on with those two, anyway? Amanda knew Browning was as insincere as a man could get when it came to females.

Had Amanda and Grant had a falling out? Was she just trying to make Carrie's brother jealous? If so, it was his guess she was succeeding better than the National League succeeded in the championship game against the Association this year, which they'd won with a hurrah. He shook his head slightly. He'd thought she had better sense.

Carrie hurried past him with a china plate piled high with slices of buttered pumpkin bread. The spicy odor blended with her flowery perfume in a tempting combination. The loud laughs and buzz of conversation continued among the men while she placed the plate on a round, marble-topped table in the middle of the room. Men grabbed for the food, but the conversation didn't falter for a moment.

He wondered how any man could see Carrie enter a room without giving her his full attention, even if, as now, she was only a month away from having a child. If there was a more beautiful woman on the planet, he'd not met her.

He stopped Carrie on her way past him, smiling down at her. "Stay with me."

He thought for a moment she would refuse, insisting she must be doing something in the kitchen, in the manner women have when there's company about. He was glad when after a moment's hesitation she nodded.

He slipped his arm about her enlarged waist, drawing her close to his side. She rested her weight against him in the familiar manner that always made him feel he hadn't been quite whole without her.

A small sigh slipped from her soft pink lips, and her head touched his shoulder. He pressed a discreet kiss to her temple. "Tired, me love?"

She gave him a little smile, but didn't answer. He supposed she was always tired these days.

"Look!" He nodded toward a pile of blue and red beneath a small table at the end of the rosewood couch. Benjy was sound asleep, his blue-clad bottom up in the air. "How can he sleep with all this noise?"

"I expect he's inherited your hearing abilities. After all, his father thinks the sound of an overflowing ball ground is as soothing as the sound of the river to most people."

He chuckled at her comparison, contentment flowing over him. He had more than any man should expect out of life. A wonderful wife, a strapping son, a vocation that was nearer his heart than anything but his family, and friends enough to fill a parlor. What more could a man want?

"Riley, old man," Browning called over the din to get his attention. "Hear you went East to see Providence play the Mets for the World's Series*."

"That's right. Mullane and I went together."

"Is Hoss Radbourne's hurling everything it's talked up to be?"

"And then some. He walked away with the series; his club barely had to help. The hurlers in this room are going to be hard put to keep up with those clubs who use Radbourne's overhand pitch when it's legalized in the Association next season."

Hoots from the Browns' hurlers greeted his statement.

"Riley's right," Mullane agreed. "I plan to spend the winter learning Radbourne's throw. Has a lot more power and speed to it than the underhand toss, as you might guess from his sixty-win season and the way National League batting averages tumbled last year. Suggest you men spend the winter practicing up, too." He grinned. "Unless you don't mind losing

* Different from the World Series of today. It was decided each year whether a World's Series would be held.

to my club, that is."

"And what club might that be by this time next year?" Dexter asked with a laugh. "You were with Louisville two years ago, played with us last year, then turned traitor and moved on to the Toledo Blue Stockings. Never know where you'll show up."

"What's a man to do but move on when he's sampled all the women the town has to offer?" Mullane winked broadly at Amanda, who laughed at him.

"Heard you aren't too popular in Toledo," Charlie offered, his gaze on the slice of pumpkin bread in his big hands. "Heard you stole one of your clubmate's women."

Jeers filled the room.

Mullane's exaggerated shrug lifted his out-of-fashion, thread-bare, once-brown shirt. His broad hands spread in a gesture of defeat. "How does a gentleman turn down a lady's attentions? I was tryin' ta avoid hurtin' her feelings."

Guffaws met his claim of innocence.

The others obviously didn't believe Mullane any more than he did, Dexter thought. The scene turned Dexter's stomach as effectually as a drink of sour milk. Tony played as dirty in love as Comiskey played on the ball grounds. In spite of the unwritten code that no player poached on a woman a clubmate was courting, the men here treated the matter as a joke. Most likely the other player and woman involved didn't feel that way.

He liked Mullane as a player, and usually enjoyed his company, but not when he was like this. Never did like seeing a man treat women as though they were toys made for men. A number of the players were womanizers, but Mullane and Browning were two of the worst. His glance rested on Amanda's laughing face, flushed with excitement, and uneasiness snaked through him. Was she scheduled to be Mullane's next victim?

"Planning to use the flat-sided bat next season?" Grant asked.

Was Grant trying to change the conversation because he was as uncomfortable as he was himself with the nasty scene which had just played out before them?

Tall, slender club manager Charlie Comiskey shook his head.

"With all the changes the leagues are hurling at us this season, sport won't be the same."

Looking at him, Dexter wondered what was ahead for their club with Comiskey leading it. He'd rather liked their last manager, but couldn't blame him for leaving after all the brawling between club members. The former manager had told him he'd "rather tackle a hundred angry water works customers than a solitary St. Louis base baller—especially when the slugger is drunk and in possession of the idea that it is his solemn duty to slug the manager of the nine."

His glance moved among the Browns seated in his parlor: Frail-looking Bob Caruthers, the best base-running hurler in the profession, but a ladies' man, to put it delicately; Scottish, fleet-footed Hugh Nicol, with a strength that belied his five-foot-four-inch frame, who thought nothing of incurring his clubmate's wrath by passing them on the basepaths when they'd batted before him; Arlie Latham, a quick, talented player, but with a mouth so foul some of the kranks came to the ball park only to hear him abuse the members of the opposing club; Pat Deasley, talented catcher, but a heavy drinker and envied by his clubmates for his club-high salary; Jumbo McGinnis, a good pitcher and possibly his favorite of the Browns group, a huge boy of twenty with a heart of gold, a family man like himself with a year-old daughter. No angels in the group, but on the field they put aside everything else and pulled together for the glory of the Browns.

He liked each of them, when they weren't drunk or just generally acting like fools, which they did far too often. If they would put their immature tempers and jealousies behind them, the Browns just might make a decent club next year.

"I figure hitting and kicking's as much a part of the sport as pitching, striking, and catching," Comiskey said slowly. "You might all want to keep that in mind, especially with the changes in hurling and other rules. Me, I don't aim to be party to a losing ball club."

Discomfort walked through the room, leaving silence behind. *So that's what it will be like with Comiskey in charge*, Dexter thought. His words were a warning to the Browns, he knew. Those here would be expected to pass the advice to their clubmates: win at any price. Well, here was one player who wouldn't play by that motto, even if it cost him his position.

His glance shifted to Carrie. She was staring at Charlie with her lovely lips open slightly, too stunned for once to comment. An uncomfortable thought startled him. He had a wife and child to support, and another child on the way; he couldn't be careless with his position. He'd have to perform better than ever to avoid being forced into cheap plays to keep his berth on the club.

"Say." Browning pitched his voice loud enough to drown out all the kranks in Sportsman's Park, as usual, and the entire room gave him their attention.

"What do you think about those Sabbatarians? They've been out strong this year. Think they might get Sunday ball canceled?"

"Eastern teams would like that," Dexter replied, "since most of their hometowns have laws against playing on Sundays. They end up in matches away from home on Sundays." The topic of Sunday ball made him a little uneasy. He hadn't been to church with Carrie much in the last few months, and he didn't like the guilt he felt when the topic was broached.

"Von der Ahe calls kranks 'fans' for their fanatical devotion to Base Ball. Appears to me the term more aptly applies to the Sabbatarians," someone volunteered.

Mullane chuckled. "Did you hear about the Columbus-Indianapolis match the Sabbatarians pushed the police to break up? Police arrived at the grounds, all right, but waited to watch the Columbus Buckeyes win over the Brooklyn Grays before arresting both clubs."

Dexter felt Carrie stiffen and a weary dread rolled over him. Couldn't she keep her religious battles out of sight for one night?

No sense riling up the company. Not that he expected for a moment she would consider that.

She didn't. As soon as the guffaws over Mullane's story died down enough for her to be heard, she said, "It's against the law to play Sunday ball in Columbus, and the club members and their owners well knew it. Besides, a little more church and a little less Base Ball wouldn't hurt any of you, or the spectators who spend their Sundays drinking beer and watching you play."

Comiskey gave her a saucy grin. "No law against Sunday ball in this town, but sounds like you're planning to organize a division of the Sabbatarians here anyway."

Eyes flashing, she crossed her arms over the top of her baby-large stomach. "Perhaps I shall."

The room screamed with silence. The men stared first at her, then at their hands. Dexter swallowed a groan. Sunday ball was one of the Association's biggest draws. The Sabbatarians threatened the livelihood of every player in this room, but she'd never understand that.

Grant tossed a crumpled bit of newspaper at Comiskey, grinning when the man looked up at him. "Guess nobody warned you our father is a minister."

Comiskey gave him an uncharacteristically sheepish smile. "No, no one did."

The others gave nervous laughs and began conversing again.

Dexter let out a sigh of relief. All he needed was to have volatile Von der Ahe hear a rumor about Carrie organizing a chapter of the Sabbatarians in Der Boss's back yard! Carrie wouldn't need to worry then about Sunday matches keeping him from church. He'd be tossed out on his ear, and not be playing any day of the week. Not be paid either. W*onder whether her religious fervor would disappear when there wasn't any food for us or the little ones!*

The atmosphere never regained its former comfort, and half an hour later Mullane convinced the others to adjourn to Von der Ahe's saloon near the Sportsman's Park for the remainder of the evening "since Grandmother Riley doesn't believe in servin' men's drinks in his house, and refuses to pay the bill at his brother's saloon."

The comment was accompanied by a friendly grin, as references to his refusal to drink always were. The other base ballers seldom called him Grandmother, Parson, or Deacon, as they did other non-drinking players. He never preached at them to give up the bottle. He knew they were glad enough for his sober state when their legs wouldn't support them any longer and they needed assistance getting to their beds. He'd played the role of caretaker for each man in this room except Grant. It wasn't a role he relished, but a man had to be loyal to his clubmates.

Alarm rang in his brain when Browning tucked Amanda's hand in the crook of his arm. Surely he wasn't planning to take her along on a drinking party!

Anger rolled over him. He could hear it in his tight voice. "We'll see Amanda home." He drew her away from Browning's side.

Pete looked from him to Amanda in surprise. "Isn't that for her to decide?"

Dexter usually didn't allow himself to show anger toward his player friends, but he deliberately made an exception this time, and knew his eyes were speaking more plainly than his low-pitched words. "She's my sister, and it's my home."

Browning stared at him for a moment, then shrugged. Turning to the sputtering Amanda, he took her hand and touched his lips to her fingers. "May I take you for a buggy ride tomorrow?"

"You may take me with you now." She tugged at her arm, trying to loose it from Dexter's grasp.

He only gripped it harder and whispered against her hair, "Don't act the fool. These men have their choice of women. It's those whose behavior demands they be treated like ladies that impress them."

He was relieved to see from her expression that his warning had the desired effect, although she was obviously still angry at his interference.

When the others had filed out, Grant said to her, "I'll take you home."

Her anger rippled out once more. "Ye'll do no sech thing! Dexter can see me home."

Dexter looked from one to the other, puzzled. The two of them had been wildly in love from the day they met. He knew his sister's temper well, but he'd never seen her turn it toward Grant. What had happened to set the two of them at odds?

Grant's usually easy-going face was stiff with repressed fury. "There's no need to take Dex from his family just because you're too proud to put up with my presence for a few minutes. He has little enough time with Carrie and Benjy, what with being out of town so often."

His argument apparently convinced her, for Amanda agreed, with obvious reluctance, to ride with him.

Watching them depart, Dexter braced a shoulder against the tall porch pillar. "Wonder what that's about?"

She shook her head. "I don't know, but surely they'll resolve it. They are so much in love."

Dexter shifted his weight, and slipped his arms about her waist from behind, smiling against her hair when his hands would barely touch. He adjusted them slightly until they rested above her own hands, above the exciting lump where her stomach usually existed. He nuzzled her neck, then whispered in her ear, "Grant is no more in love with her than I am with you. Not even close."

Her hand rested on his cheek. The softness of her skin against his sun-roughened face amazed him as it always did, and sent a thrill running along his nerves.

She sighed sweetly. "I needed to hear that tonight. I don't feel very lovable when I'm this big with the child."

"Our baby only makes you more lovable." He touched his

lips to the palm of her hand at his cheek.

"Tell me how much you love me, Dexter."

He could hear the smile in her voice. "My love is too. . .too immense to be expressed in mere words."

Her laugh was filled with relaxed, carefree joy. "That is pure blarney, Mr. Riley. Don't think you can escape answering so easily."

"My love for you is no blarney, me love." Blarney came easy. Important things were difficult to express.

Besides, women asked the silliest things. How could a person explain how much he loved someone? Didn't promising to spend her life with her show her the depth of his love? What could he possibly say to expand on that?

"Look!" She pointed at the sky. "A shooting star!"

They watched in silence while it flared and faded.

"I'm still waiting."

He'd thought she'd forgotten. Wished she had. He could no more explain his love than explain the stars.

The stars. "Can you count the stars, girleen?"

"Of course not." She laughed. "And stop trying to change the subject."

"I'm not. That sky-full of stars is how much I love you, but that one shooting star is all the love I'm able to express."

She brushed her cheek against his shoulder, and he liked the softness of her hair moving against his chin. "What a beautiful thing to say, Dexter! But. . . "

"But what?"

"If you love me so much. . . "

"Yes, me love?"

"Why do you no longer attend church, when you know how important it is to me?"

The sweetness of the moment fled. "One thing has nothing to do with the other."

"Doesn't it?" She turned to face him, pulling out of his arms. "Before we married, you promised to attend church with me whenever you were home on Sundays, but since last July, you've attended only twice."

He stuffed his hands in his trouser pockets. "I feel like a hypocrite when I go. I can't sing those songs and repeat all those phrases everyone is supposed to say about what they believe. Makes me uncomfortable, like I'm lying."

"I'm uncomfortable, too, attending without my husband. Some members have told me they are praying for you! They think you are backslidden."

"What does that mean?"

"That you aren't following the Lord anymore."

"Well, I'm not. What's so embarrassing about them thinking the truth? Is that why you're upset? You're worried about what people will think?"

"No! I'm upset because the most important thing in the world to me is for you to love the Lord."

He dragged a sigh from deep inside himself. He was so tired of arguing about his faith, or more accurately, his lack of it. "Ye've known from the beginning that I'm not even knowing whether I believe in Him. Nothing has changed."

Her eyes were large, pooled with tears that made him feel as though someone had carved up his insides.

"Everything has changed, Dexter. Maybe you don't understand that yet, but it's true. At least when you were attending church, you were hearing God's Word. Now you're refusing to allow God even that little opportunity to convince you He exists and loves you." Tears rolled over her bottom lashes to dribble down her cheeks in accusing little droplets. "Everything has changed," she whispered again.

Benjy's cry startled them. The wail stopped a second, then resumed. He recognized the cry. The boy had awakened, and was waiting for someone to come to him.

Carrie brushed past him and hurried into the house.

He dropped down on the top step, disturbing a few crisp leaves which had drifted to the porch, and ran both hands down his face. She was right. Everything had changed. He'd decided he couldn't continue acting like a hypocrite, going to church and talking and laughing with the members of the congregation when he didn't share their faith.

He hadn't expected his marriage to change because of his decision.

Carrie had tried to tell him. Way back when he'd first asked her to marry him. She'd told him the difference in their beliefs would become a wedge between them, driving them apart.

He hadn't believed it. He hadn't thought anything was powerful enough to come between them when he loved her so much. Of all things, how could her faith in a God who was supposed to be Love itself be the thing that came between them?

Of course, she'd say it wasn't her faith, but his lack of it that was the dividing force.

Either way, he didn't like what it was doing to their life together. But what could he do about it? He could hardly order her not to believe in God and wouldn't want to if he could. Her faith meant too much to her. But he couldn't make himself believe, either. He snorted, and looked up through autumn-bare branches. How did a man force himself to have faith?

The question left him feeling more hopeless and alone than a rookie hurler facing the league's top club for the first time.

nine

Carrie broached the subject of Amanda with Grant a number of times over the next few months. He refused to discuss it.

She was surprised to find Amanda was almost as reticent, since she felt they'd become close friends. "I love him, Carrie," she said in a trembling voice, her green eyes tear-studded, "but he doesn't believe we are right for each other."

When Carrie pressed her, she said she didn't think it proper to say more. "Grant is your brother, and Dexter is mine. I don't wish either of you to feel you must stand for or against me or Grant."

Carrie and Dexter reluctantly respected her stand, hurting for the couple and wishing there was a way to help them find each other again.

Nearly a year passed before Carrie discovered the reason for the couple's division. She'd been telling Grant about the celebration planned in honor of the Browns' winning the pennant.

"Amanda said everyone in the old neighborhood is as excited for Dexter as if he was a member of their own families. She's helping their oldest brother, Frank, plan a special party for him at the Irish Stars tomorrow night."

She hated Dexter's family's events, especially hated when they were held at the Irish Stars saloon, even when Frank arranged for a special street-side restaurant to be set up in front of the establishment, lit with mellow glowing gas-lights below a star-sprinkled blue awning in imitation of the city's finest cafes.

She tossed off her preoccupation and glanced at Grant, surprised he hadn't commented. She recognized the guarded look that always came to Grant's eyes at the mention of Dexter's sister, and said cautiously, "You never told me why you stopped courting Amanda."

"Didn't I?" He stared straight ahead. His hard voice didn't invite her to continue.

She did so anyway. "I thought the two of you so much in love."

It was a minute before he responded. "You're just a romantic, like most women."

She laid a hand on his forearm, staring silently at him until he looked at her. "I'm not trying to be a busy-body. I care about your happiness. It's easy to see she still loves you. You loved her, too. What happened between you?"

She watched his gaze search hers, saw the tick at the corner of his mouth when he decided to answer.

"You and Dexter happened."

Shock bolted through her. She couldn't even get out the question she knew must be showing in every inch of her face.

He rubbed his hand over hers. "I could see things weren't everything they could be between you, in spite of your love for each other. I mean, he hardly ever comes to church. You avoid talking about religious topics when he's around so you won't make him uncomfortable. All our lives it's been normal to talk about spiritual things, remember?"

She nodded slowly.

"Sometimes I. . .I feel guilty for introducing you to Dexter. Remember how you and Emmet and I would get into friendly arguments about Scripture passages, or pray together for each other? We don't do that with Dex."

She stared at the black-and-white, four-in-hand necktie above his black, three-button cut-away coat. She didn't want him to see her eyes. She longed desperately for the intimacy of sharing her spiritual life with Dexter, but hadn't realized anyone but Hannah knew how she felt, least of all Grant.

"Amanda and I couldn't share that either." His voice had softened. Cautiously, she raised her lashes to search his gaze. A sad little smile sat on his lips. "I tried to talk with her about the Lord, but she didn't want to hear about my faith. She doesn't believe in God, any more than Dexter does."

"I'm sorry."

"I'm sorry, too. I don't believe Amanda and I could have much of a life together without sharing our faith. But mostly, I wish she knew the peace that comes from trusting God, and I'm afraid for her that she might never let herself experience it."

His eyes looked ancient, and the acceptance of continual pain she saw there caused her chest to burn with empathy. She knew that particular pain; the same pain she'd lived with through three years of marriage waiting for Dexter to choose to believe in God.

"I've been courting Phoebe Wilson since opening my law practice in Riverton last spring."

"Phoebe Wilson?"

He nodded.

"Why haven't you told me before?"

"Wanted to wait until I was certain I'd continue seeing her, what with her being Emmet's sister and all."

"And are you certain?"

He nodded again, smartly. "I've decided to ask her to marry me."

"M. . .marry you?" Quiet Phoebe with the pale brown hair and reserved nature? She was as different from sparkling Amanda as the moon from the sun. Not that she wasn't pleasant, but Carrie couldn't imagine her brother looking at her with love glowing in his eyes the way it did when he looked at Amanda.

He grinned. "Cheer up. She may not have me."

"As if any woman with sense would turn you down," she championed him. "But. . .are you certain. . . ?"

"I care deeply for her, if that's what you're asking."

"As much as you love Amanda?"

It was a moment before he replied. "Not in precisely the same manner, but then, does anyone care for two people in exactly the same way? Besides, love is more than. . .emotions. Phoebe and I can have a good life together. I'll devote myself to her."

But would he spend his life with her missing Amanda? Her chest and throat burned with the thought of a future for him without the woman he truly loved.

However, it was painful, too, living with Dexter when they didn't share the bond of faith. Grant apparently was looking at the possibility of both pains, and choosing the one least difficult for him.

Fear and despair twisted together, joined cruel strength, and constricted her heart. Things had changed between her and Dexter in the last year or so. The joy had been replaced with tension. Sometimes she even wondered whether Dexter still loved her.

Perhaps Grant had made the wiser choice.

❧

"Quite a day! St. Louis is batty about you Browns!"

Dexter grinned his agreement of Tony Mullane's comment, as they followed Carrie, Benjy, and the neighbor boy, Joey, into the house. Hadn't stopped grinning all day, he admitted to himself. Same way yesterday, when they arrived back in the city on the special train decorated with flags and the huge banner emblazoned "St. Louis Browns, Champions 1885." Half the population had been waiting at the depot to congratulate them.

"They deserve the attention, after the way they've played their hearts out for Mr. Von der Ahe this year."

Carrie's fierce statement surprised him and warmed him all the way through. He'd been afraid they were growing apart this last year, and he hadn't known how to stop it. Sometimes, he'd even wondered whether she still cared for him.

He'd thought for awhile she was simply worn out from the baby, but Margaret was almost ten months old now.

Perhaps it was his fault, this distancing. He knew he'd put up some barriers against her constant pestering to get him to believe.

When he'd asked before they married whether she was embarrassed by his vocation as a base baller, she'd insisted she wasn't. Something had changed. He was certain she was embarrassed by him now. Maybe when he completed his degree, put Base Ball behind him, and became a counselor at law, she'd not find their marriage distasteful.

He'd been celebrating with the club and the kranks for two days and two nights, but she was the only one with whom he truly wanted to celebrate—at least, he wanted to celebrate with the woman she'd been when they married.

He watched her attempting without much success to collect the lads' jackets and hats. The little tikes were still excited about the exhibition game and Buffalo Bill's Wild West Show they'd seen at Statesman's Park that afternoon. Von der Ahe had gone all out to celebrate their pennant win. All the way home, the boys had been going back and forth between playing cowboys and base ballers. At that, he reflected, cowboys were probably the only men who led a life as independent and free of restrictions as base ballers.

In spite of the boys' chatter, the house felt empty without little Margaret. He'd be glad when she was home from Carrie's parents' tomorrow.

"Mr. Riley."

Dexter looked down to see frail-looking, six-year-old Joey staring up at him solemnly. *If he were a puppy, he'd be the runt of the litter*, he thought irrelevantly. "Have a good time today?"

A smile filled the skinny face. "Oh, yes, Mr. Riley! It was the best day of my entire life!"

"Mine too." He glanced across the room at Carrie, still trying to relieve Benjy of his jacket. "Well, almost." Nothing compared to the day he met Carrie, except maybe the day she first said she loved him.

"Mr. Riley, could you teach me ta be a base baller?"

Mullane shouted with laughter. "Have a mighty bit of growin' ta do before ya can be a base baller!"

Dexter shoved an elbow in Mullane's side. "Don't mind him. He's just jealous of you 'cause he's so tall he has to look down at almost everyone else on the planet. You don't have to be tall to start learning how to play. I started playing right about your age."

"Really?"

"Just with the neighbor kids, of course."

Joey's thin eyebrows met. "Oh. The other kids won't let me play. They say I'm too small."

"Tell you what. You come over every day I'm in town, and I'll practice with you. After I've taught you a few things, I bet the others will be fighting over which club you join."

"Wow! Thanks, Mr. Riley!"

The men sat in the parlor chatting companionably while Carrie settled the boys into bed. She'd been wise to tell Joey's mother he could stay over night with them, considering what a long day it turned out to be.

She joined them in the parlor later, and he got a sinking feeling in his stomach when he saw her frown at the fat cigar clenched in Mullane's lips. He knew she didn't care for the odor, but he was so glad Mullane wasn't drinking today, that he wasn't about to complain about the cigar.

He was relieved when she didn't mention it, either, but simply offered them coffee and cookies. His Base Ball friends and even his brother, Frank, seldom visited at their home any more. He couldn't blame them. He'd observed their discomfort at his wife's caustic remarks concerning Sunday ball and drinking among kranks and players. Carrie had stopped suggesting dinner parties involving his friends and family, other than Amanda, whom she still welcomed. Besides, her afternoons and evenings were so full of church activities, there wasn't much time available to entertain friends.

He'd come to dread the pinched, prim look about her lips, the martyr-attitude she wore like a funeral dress when around his favorite acquaintances.

He studied Mullane, who was reliving an especially difficult play made during the match that day. Drinking was beginning to take its toll. Tony's stomach was a little too large and round for his tall frame. Puffy bags of flesh beneath his eyes, and a florid complexion marred the famed good looks.

Why did so many men refuse to recognize the cost they paid for what they considered enjoyment? He counted too many of his friends among that group. Grant was one of the few who didn't drink or womanize. Of course, his strong faith kept him from such things.

His attention was distracted finally at Mullane's mention of a wager he'd made. When Carrie returned with refreshments, they were laughing so hard they were holding their sides.

"What is so humorous?"

"Fresh Arlie," Dexter managed to choke out.

She wrinkled her nose in distaste. "That awful third baseman who is always in trouble for his foul language?"

"The same," Mullane confirmed cheerfully.

"Did you see the race before the exhibition game?" Dexter asked. "Arlie was sure no one in either major league could run faster than himself, that he put up a challenge to pay any player who could outrun him."

Mullane pulled the cigar from his lips. "It was a beautiful sight ta see, Billy Sunday whippin' past him that way. Can that man move!"

"Sunday. What an inappropriate name for a ball player."

The laughter inside Dexter died at her sarcastic tone.

He noticed Mullane's grin didn't decrease the length of a fairy's footstep, as his grandmother used to say. "You joined those Sabbatarians yet?" Tony challenged her.

"Only in spirit, unfortunately."

About the only religious-related organization she hadn't

joined yet, Dexter thought.

"Does Cincinnati allow Sunday ball? That is the club on which you play, is it not?"

Mullane's guffaw indicated he hadn't noticed the barb in her question. "Guess you weren't payin' much mind ta the match today, Mrs. Riley. I was hurlin' for the Cincinnati Reds against the Browns."

"Well, do they play Sunday ball in Cincinnati?"

"Yep. Draw the best crowds of the week on Sunday."

Better try to change the subject before she gets up on her soap box, Dexter thought. "Surprised you were allowed to pitch today, Mullane, since you were suspended the entire season."

Tony shrugged with his usual good nature. "It was just an exhibition match. Season is officially over." He crushed the cigar stub onto the edge of one of Carrie's best china plates. Dexter watched her cringe, relieved she didn't upbraid their guest. Mullane rested his arm along the ornately carved walnut sofa frame. "Be nice ta make a salary again. Can't thank you enough for the help over the last few months."

Dexter waved his thanks away. It made him decidedly uneasy having Tony bring it up. "You'd lend me funds if I needed them."

He caught Carrie's surprised look. He hoped she wouldn't say anything and embarrass all of them. He supposed he should have told her about the loan, but. . .

"I never understood why you were suspended," she said, and Dexter felt his relief escape in a sigh. When had he become so uncomfortable about her actions around his friends? "You didn't break any of the rules, did you?"

Mullane grinned his usual self-confident grin. "Only one: I wanted more money. That's the worst thing a player can do, accordin' ta the owners."

Dexter shook his head. "Owners just don't want players moving from one club to another every year. Weakens the clubs."

"The owners don't give a hill of beans for the clubs' health.

All they care about is their pocketbooks. I've played with four clubs in as many years, and made more money each time I changed. That's what scares the owners."

"You're only bitter," Dexter argued.

"Mark my words, there's rumors of a salary cap comin'"

They argued the issue until all three of them were too tired to continue and Mullane left for his hotel.

Alone in their room, Dexter's exhaustion fled when he slid his arms around Carrie's waist and drew her into his arms, lowering his lips to hers. She didn't resist his kiss. She never did, but he couldn't honestly say she responded to his kiss either. He couldn't recall the last time she'd kissed him back.

Loneliness swelled through him, filling him until he thought he couldn't bear it. How could a man feel lonely with the woman he loved in his arms?

"I've missed you."

The words didn't say half of it. He'd missed her company and her arms while away on the last trip. But more, he missed the part of her she'd deliberately pulled further and further away from him over the last year. He missed the way she used to lean into his arms with complete abandonment, lifting her lips eagerly to his. He missed the way she'd delighted in his presence, laughed easily with him, shared the smallest parts of her days and her deepest dreams.

"I've missed you, too."

She could as well be saying, "I made dinner this evening," for all the passion in the words, he thought, frustrated.

Desire to have her respond to his arms as she used to made him prolong his kisses. He teased at her lips with tiny, tender pecks, lifted a hand to the back of her neck, then higher to play his fingers through her thick hair. He kept his kisses gentle, whispering his love between each touch, longing for her to return his passion.

Her lips remained stiff, her arms cool.

He closed his eyes and rubbed his chin over the top of her head, swallowing his disappointment. "Only one trip left this year. We go to Chicago next week to play the National League champs. Come with me."

She shook her head against his shoulder. The waves of her hair brushed against his hands seductively. "I can't. What would I do with Benjy and Margaret?"

The tone of her voice told him she hadn't for a moment considered the question serious, but he continued to press her. "Your mother or Amanda would watch them." He wanted to keep his face hidden from her so she couldn't see how important this was to him, but for that very reason, he forced himself to look directly into her eyes. "It's the first match I'll ever play in between the two major Base Ball leagues. I want you there."

He knew the moment she realized he was serious. She pulled back from his arms, straightened her dress, and crossed to her vanity to reach for her hair brush. "It's out of the question." Her voice was crisp and efficient. "There's not only the children to consider, you know I'm in charge of the Ladies' Needlework Society at church. We've a special entertainment scheduled for next week to raise funds. I missed an important planning session to attend the festivities for the Browns today. I cannot possibly miss the event, also."

And when are we to be scheduled? he wondered, watching her pull the pearl-handled brush through the hair that fell like a glossy black cape about her shoulders.

At least in Base Ball there was always another opportunity, he thought, if not this year, then next. But when that special fire between a man and a woman went out, it couldn't always be rekindled. Maybe it was already too late; maybe Carrie no longer cared.

At the thought, he recognized the sinking feeling he always got in his gut when the Browns were behind and the umpire called the match game's final out.

ten

1887

Why did she have this sinking feeling in her stomach, Carrie wondered, watching the shiny, flower-bedecked coach carry away Grant and his new bride, Phoebe. A wedding ought to be a happy occasion. Certainly the bride and groom appeared overjoyed. So why wasn't she?

Two years had passed since Grant asked Phoebe to marry him. She should have been accustomed to the idea of them together by now.

"Faith, and it be strange to think of Grant married to someone other than Amanda. I kept hoping they'd patch things up."

She nodded at Dexter's comment. He must be more upset than he appeared outwardly over the wedding. His Irish accent was stronger than usual today.

"Ye look mighty handsome in your black suit with the yellow rose and streamers, Mr. Riley. 'Tis a fine lookin' groomsman ye be."

He laughed, as she'd hoped he would, at her poor attempt to imitate the Irish. A ribbon of regret wound through her. They so seldom laughed together anymore.

Yet her compliment was true. As usual, women's gazes had followed him about during the reception. Ladies had eagerly hung on their escorts' arms when the men had stopped to speak of Base Ball to the now famous player.

Margaret leaned against his leg, patting the black material with a chubby almost three-year-old palm. "Han'some."

Dexter lifted the girl into his arms and smiled into Carrie's eyes. "All the Riley women are full of Irish blarney today." The smile gentled. "You look tired. Why don't I take these two youngsters home? I know you want to help your mother with a few things before coming home yourself."

She nodded, grateful for his thoughtfulness. "That would be nice. Things will go quicker without the children to watch."

She saw him glance over her shoulder briefly, but paid it no mind. She kissed the children good-bye. When she straightened, she was surprised at Dexter's peck on her cheek.

"I love you," he whispered, his warm breath fanning the tiny curls in front of her ear. Her heart gave an unusual little jolt. He seldom spoke those words in public any more. Or in private, for that matter. When they were first married he'd whispered them everywhere they went.

She watched him go down the wide steps to the street with the children, then turned to re-enter through the huge oak doors the church her father served. She stopped short. Emmet stood there, watching her over the shoulders of departing guests.

Had Emmet been the reason for Dexter's small show of affection? Was it possible her husband was jealous of her former suitor?

Emmet nodded at an elderly couple directly in front of him, and approached her. She felt suddenly light-headed, wanting to speak with him, wondering what she could say, wondering what he felt toward her.

His face was as wide and plain as ever beneath the mouse-brown hair that had receded slightly in the five years since she'd married Dexter. He stopped two feet away from her, smiling down with friendly eyes. "Hello, Carrie. You look lovely. I always did like you in blue."

He greeted me as casually as though we'd seen each other only yesterday. "You look well, also."

He couldn't know—no one must know—the way her heartbeat had quickened earlier that day when she'd looked in her mirror after dressing. She knew he would be at his sister's wedding and couldn't help but wonder what he would think of the way she looked in her new gown with its fitted waist and huge, fashionable bustle that made her more shapely than she was in truth.

"Are you happy, Carrie?"

"I. . .as much as I have any right to be, I expect." Especially considering she was wondering whether she had married the wrong man! She missed Emmet's friendship, the easy way they had together, the way she'd been able to share anything with him, and especially the many long, exciting conversations about the Lord and the Bible. Her relationship with Dexter seemed shallow by comparison.

Had she confused passion for love in marrying Dexter?

"You have a fine looking family. Only the two children?"

She nodded. There weren't likely to be any more if things didn't improve between her and Dexter. Dexter's chaste kiss a few minutes earlier was his only intimate touch in months. They took pains to avoid romantic gestures of late.

"I understand Mr. Von der Ahe named some apartment buildings for the Browns' players after they out-played Chicago, the National League Champs, last year. You must be proud of your husband."

"Of course." She searched for another topic of conversation, almost afraid she'd blurt out the truth about her miserable marriage. "Phoebe said you've not married yet."

He shook his head slightly, his smile not changing. "No. Haven't found a woman who will have me."

It was on the tip of her tongue to say she had made a foolish mistake in not marrying him. Her chest ached with the effort to keep the words inside. She knew he wouldn't want to hear them, and she wouldn't much like herself for saying them, either. To put the thought into words would demean them both. She'd vowed to be faithful to Dexter for life.

"I've been offered a pastorate. Did Phoebe tell you?"

"No. Where?"

"A small church in North Carolina." His gaze dropped to his feet. When it met hers again a moment later, it was slightly less open than before, though he continued to smile. "It will be quite a new experience, in the mountains and all." He shrugged one shoulder. "I thought it would be good for me to move away from this area. The congregation preferred a married man, but evidently none of the married men they asked accepted the call."

She studied the pearl buttons running up her elbow-length gloves and fought down the feeling of loss flooding through her. She could have been the wife of a pastor—how she would have loved that! Instead she was married to a base baller who did not even believe in God.

"Perhaps the Lord has a woman waiting there for you—the future Mrs. Emmet Wilson."

He didn't respond.

When she looked up, she caught the longing in his gaze, and it brought tears to her eyes.

"Perhaps." His whisper cracked.

She should leave now, but she couldn't seem to pull herself away.

He licked his lips. Was he as nervous as she?

"I pray for you and your husband every day."

"You do?"

He nodded. "That the Lord will bless both of you in your marriage. And for your husband's salvation. Has he found the Lord yet?"

She looked away, ashamed. "No."

He touched her elbow, then immediately removed his hand, and she knew he was uncomfortable with his impulsive act.

"Don't give up on him, Carrie. God won't." One corner of his straight, thin lips lifted in a smile, but his eyes remained sad. "Look with whom God has allowed him to share life. He must love Dexter a great deal."

Guilt poured through her, burning like hot cooking oil. Emmet was such a fine man. She was glad she hadn't given voice to her baser emotions.

"There you are!"

Carrie jerked in surprise at her mother's voice. The middle-aged woman bustled toward them, her elegant mauve gown of watered silk rustling, pointed shiny black toes flashing out from the beneath the skirt. Her hand enveloped Carrie's. "I know you'll excuse us, Emmet. There's so much to be done."

Carrie murmured a hasty good-bye over her shoulder and followed her mother inside.

Glad there was no remonstrance forthcoming for her unseemly behavior in speaking alone with a man who once courted her, she immediately went to work helping her mother collect the flowers and satin bows decorating the sanctuary. The large room was thick with the smell of yellow and white roses.

Twenty minutes later she and her parents stood before the altar, and surveyed the sanctuary.

"Do we have everything?" Carrie asked.

"Yes." Her mother's double chin plumped when she nodded her head. "Maybe I'd best check the reception hall downstairs, one more time."

While they waited for her, Carrie ran her fingers along the smooth altar rail, staring up at the huge painting of Jesus praying in the garden. She'd always loved that picture; it had such a serene quality. But she knew from the Bible story it depicted that Christ hadn't felt serene that night. Had He felt as tired as she did now? "Don't give up on him," Emmet had said of Dexter. She almost had given up, she realized. She was too fatigued to keep fighting for Dexter and their marriage.

Her father leaned back against the rail beside her.

She took a long, shaky breath. "You were right, you know, about Dexter and me."

"What are you talking about?" She could hear the frown in his voice.

"Remember telling me that believers couldn't be happy married to nonbelievers? You were right."

Her father swallowed hard. She supposed she was making him uncomfortable with her confession, but now that she'd started, she wanted to continue.

"I made the wrong choice when I married Dexter. I thought if I had enough faith, God would find a way to reach Dexter's heart. If anything, he's further from God than on our wedding day."

She turned to her father, and saw tears in his gray eyes, before her own vision blurred. "He hasn't gone to church in three years except at Easter and Christmas, as you well know. He avoids even saying grace at meals, asking the children to say it instead. And you've heard of the Browns' awful exploits this year. It's horrid to think about the kind of people with whom he associates, and to whom he exposes the children." She sniffed loudly. "So you see, you were right. I should have married a Christian. I should have married Emmet."

She surrendered to the sobs that welled up inside her. Her father rubbed one hand on her back, and she wondered whether he who gave guidance to so many felt at a loss to comfort his daughter.

"You're probably right," her father agreed when her sobs had finally slowed to jerky breaths and unladylike sniffles. "Since the Bible warns us not to marry unbelievers, it probably *was* God's will that you marry a man like Emmet who shares your faith."

Carrie dabbed a woefully inadequate square of heather-scented linen at her nose and sniffed. "What can I do? I can't divorce him."

"No, I don't believe that would be God's will, either. When we purposely choose to act in defiance of God's Word, we have to live with the consequences. I have no way of knowing what the consequences will be during the years you spend with Dexter. But I know that if you ask God's forgiveness for acting against His Word, and ask Him to guide you from this point on, He will do so. Shall we pray together?"

Her father put a comforting arm about her when they knelt at the altar rail. "Dear Father God," her father began in the deep voice that could rumble through the sanctuary like thunder on a

Sunday morning, "thank Thee for this daughter Thou hast given us to love, and for Dexter, whom Thou hast allowed to love her, and be loved by her. We long for the day when he shall know Thee, and thank Thee that Thou wilt not quit asking for his heart. We ask Thee to teach Carrie how to love this man she has vowed to Thee to cherish forever. Show her where she must change, and assist her in so doing. In Thy Son's name, Amen."

Fury routed self-pity from her veins. "Change me?" she demanded.

Her father stood up calmly and offered her a hand to help her rise. "Well, it's obvious you can't do anything to change Dexter. Isn't that what you've been trying to do for the last five years?"

Her hands balled into fists. "But I'm the Christian! Why should I be the one to change? If he becomes a believer, everything will be fine."

Her father bent his head, lifted shaggy black-and-gray brows, and peered at her over the top of his wire-rimmed spectacles. "A common misconception, that becoming a Christian solves all life's problems. Believe me, I've spoken with enough unhappily married Christians to know. Every one of us still has a lot of changing to do after we accept Christ's salvation."

"But there is nothing wrong with me that needs changing! I tell you, the problem is Dexter. I've tried everything I know to make him a believer."

Her father nodded. "Except changing yourself."

Speechless with rage, she rushed down the aisle and out of the church to await her parents in her father's buggy.

She had humbled herself before him, allowing him to see what a mess she'd made in defying him and God to marry Dexter. And what was his response? Loving sympathy for her plight? No! Instead he advised her—*her*, a woman who had followed the Christian faith all her life—he advised *her* to change!

eleven

Why had she invited her parents over to help celebrate her and Dexter's fifth anniversary? Carrie asked herself for the tenth time that day. She had a throbbing headache. It had started before she got out of bed that morning, and grown worse every hour. It made it difficult to act civil toward anyone.

No, that wasn't true. It wasn't just the headache.

She'd been irritable ever since Grant's wedding last week. Discussing and praying over the situation with her parents had made everything worse. Now it wasn't only she and Dexter who didn't get along, but she was so angry with her parents that her teeth clenched just thinking of them.

Which act only made her head pound all the more.

So did the boys screaming out behind the house. Dexter's offer two years ago to teach Joey to play ball had grown into a neighborhood effort since the other boys discovered one of the St. Louis Browns would take time to teach them, and her yard was their favorite ball ground. After all, one of the older boys had explained to her, Mr. Riley was out of town with the club so often, that the boys had to be around in hopes of catching him when he was home.

They caught him all too often. At first she'd been pleased to see him show an interest in the boys. She'd actually thought it an endearing trait! But she'd had no intention of all but adopting a dozen loud boys.

A "thunk" was quickly followed by the sound of the back wall reverberating from a solid hit by a base ball. She threw shut the kitchen window as cheers and jeers were raised in the yard.

She hadn't expected the broken windows, chipped paint, or

destroyed flowers and vegetables that came with the small base ballers, either. She grabbed her head. The pounding had definitely worsened.

The grandfather clock in the front hall sent its booming message through the house. She groaned. Did everything have to thunk or pound or boom today? Five o'clock. Her parents would be here any minute, and the new cook had only begun the meal.

Dexter came in from the yard, slamming the back door behind him. "Hello!"

She gritted her teeth and went to the pantry for a blue spatterware pan. When she returned, Dexter was staring out the window with a freshly pumped glass of water in one hand.

He must have heard her crossing the floor, for he said without turning around, "I'm worried about Joey. He's too skinny for eight. His veins show blue through his skin. Think he could be sickly?"

"When he's about eighteen he'll suddenly turn muscular like all the rest of you men."

He did turn from the window at that, with the laugh she so seldom saw anymore twinkling in his green eyes. He set the glass on the counter and slipped his arms about her waist, nuzzling her neck. "All the better to take care of our womenfolk."

She pushed him away impatiently. "My parents will be here soon." After hardly touching her in months, why had he started again during the last week?

Drawing water from the pump beside the iron sink into the spatterware pan, she cringed at the high pitched creak the pump handle gave. She dropped the pan into the sink with a clatter and grabbed her head. "Can't you oil that?"

She hated her petulant whine, but hated, too, that he'd been too busy playing Base Ball with the boys to maintain the pump.

He was at her side instantly. "Does your head hurt?"

"It's been throbbing all day. That noisy pump doesn't help it."

"Where's the cook? She should be doing this, not you. That's what we hired her for."

"She's helping the new maid, Jane, prepare the dining room. I told her I'd start the potatoes."

He kissed her temple, and she closed her eyes, struggling not to shove him away.

"Why don't you lie down for a few minutes? I'll bring you a cold cloth for your head, and—"

"How can I lie down when my parents are coming, and the children aren't even cleaned up yet? Benjy is bound to be a mess after playing Base Ball in the muddy yard."

"Your parents will understand if dinner is a few minutes late." He grinned. "If anyone is starved, we can always start with the cake while the rest of the meal cooks. Your mother is bringing us a cake for our anniversary, isn't she?"

She just glared at him.

He took her arm and urged her toward the door. "You're laying down and that's that. I'll clean up Benjy and Margaret." He glanced down at his sweaty brown shirt. "And me."

"But—"

"No buts. If you lie down without complaining, I'll wake you in half-an-hour."

She was glad she finally gave in. The cold cloth he brought for her forehead felt wonderful, and after the short rest, she did feel better.

Her parents didn't murmur a whit at dinner being served later than normal—and they didn't begin with the cake. They'd completed the rest of the meal and were eating the lemon pound cake piled high with whipped cream when there was a knock on the front door.

Carrie wasn't surprised that their visitor was Joey; their house was his second home. He was unusually patient with Benjy. The two of them spent most of their hours together with willow bats over their shoulders and at least one of their pockets bulging from a big ball.

Curiosity tickled at her over the tall, narrow item he carried, which was covered with a pretty blue cloth. Mischief and pride mingled in his slender face beneath pale blonde hair.

Dexter grinned from ear to ear and asked Joey to set the item on the floor beside her. When the boy had done so, he said, "Happy Anniversary, Carrie."

She slowly lifted the cloth cover. A beautiful trill greeted her. "A canary! Oh, Dexter, I've always wanted one!" Tears sprang to her eyes.

Joey's excited laugh showed how thrilled he was to be in on such a successful surprise. Beside him, Benjy jumped up and down, clapping his hands. Margaret grasped Carrie's knees and tried to push past the energetic boys to see what had excited them.

Carrie barely noticed the din the children caused. She truly had wanted a canary since she was a child and had seen one in a parishioner's home. Now, when their marriage was an absolute shambles, her husband gave her this precious gift.

It brightened the rest of the evening for her and for the children, who couldn't be budged from its cage. But it didn't keep the interest of the other adults for long. While admonishing the children not to open the cage under any circumstances, Carrie overheard Dexter telling her parents about some work he was planning on the house.

Her father gave him a friendly pat on the shoulder. "Won't embarrass you by saying this more than once, but I thank God for giving our daughter such a good husband. Not all men take such care of their wives and children. Built her this fine home. Never degrade the name you gave her by dragging it through the mud the way so many base ballers have done themselves and their families. It's a blessing to have a son-in-law like you, and that's a fact."

Was her father saying that to remind her that he thought she was the one who needed to change? Well, Dexter certainly seemed to be eating it up. He was ruddy from the unusual praise, and looked embarrassedly modest, but knowing him as she did she could see he was pleased. No wonder. He hadn't often received such compliments from her parents. Likely he still recalled the way her father had argued against their marriage.

If only I had listened to his warning! Both she and Dexter were miserable because she'd been so stubborn.

"Appreciate the money you gave toward repairing the church roof last month, too," her father continued. "Thanks to you, that's one bill that's paid off."

Carrie stared at Dexter in surprise. He hadn't told her he'd given money for the roof. He hadn't even been underneath that roof since Easter services last spring. She'd mentioned the need to him, but she'd never expected him to contribute to it.

The conversation drifted onto other topics, and eventually she remembered Emmet's news. She told her parents of his plans to shepherd a church in North Carolina. "Doesn't that sound exciting?"

Her parents agreed enthusiastically, and asked a storm of questions she couldn't answer. "You'll have to wait until Grant and Phoebe return from their honeymoon trip and ask her about her brother's plans," she said with a laugh.

Dexter's gaze snagged hers. He no longer looked pleased, but contemplated her with a darkly curious stare, as though frightened by something he saw in her. But that was silly. What could possibly frighten him?

The look was still there when her parents had left, the children in bed, and the canary's cage covered for the evening. She had just pulled the pins from her hair and begun to brush it when he came up behind her, and their gazes met in the long narrow vanity mirror.

His hands gently pulled her hair back over her shoulders. The unexpected move, so reminiscent of the early days of their marriage, made her throat ache in longing for happier times. "I like it when you wear your hair down."

He'd said that often. Still, she seldom wore it down. It was less work to wear it up; it didn't get in the way of her work, and it stayed cleaner. Besides, it wasn't considered proper for a woman her age to wear her hair down in public.

He searched her gaze in the mirror, with that same quizzical look he'd been watching her with all evening. "What is it?"

He didn't pretend to misunderstand. "Do ye ever wish ye'd married Emmet Wilson?"

Her heart stopped. Plunged on faster than ever. She tugged her hair back over one shoulder and brushed furiously. "What a silly question."

"Is it?"

She concentrated on her hair, refusing to meet his gaze again.

His hands at her shoulders gently but firmly turned her about. He took the brush from her and set it on the vanity. "Ye think I'm not a good enough man for ye, don't ye?"

"Of course not!" But it was true, and she hated the truth of it, despised herself for feeling superior to her own husband because he wasn't a Christian.

One of his crooked, callused hands cupped her cheek. She avoided his eyes as long as she could. When she finally made herself look into them, she knew he saw the truth in her face, and was ashamed it was there for him to see.

"I'm sorry I haven't made ye happy these five years." His voice was so uncharacteristically and incredibly gentle that she could feel the pain in it. "I only wish. . .that ye could love me, just as I am."

"I do!" She pressed her hand to the hand against her cheek, eager for him to understand. "I don't want you to change at all, except. . . "

"Except?"

"Except I want you to love Jesus."

He shook his head slowly. "Can't be seeing that becoming a Christian *would* change me?"

"But only in—"

He continued as though she hadn't spoken. "I used to be

thinkin' I was too honest to pretend to believe in God, even to be winning your heart. But not anymore." A rough tipped thumb traced her cheekbone. "I love ye so much, Carrie. If I thought pretending to believe would make things right between us, I'd pretend. But pretending won't help, will it?"

"If you'd just *try*—"

He tugged firmly at the hand she still clutched. She released it reluctantly, for it was as if he was pulling away his will for their marriage to work, and it terrified her to think he might be giving up on them. Strange, when *she'd* thought she had given up on them lately.

He turned back at the door. "If it was a Christian husband ye wanted, ye should have married Emmet Wilson. He wouldn't have had to change to win your love."

In stunned disbelief, she watched him leave. Moments later, she heard the front door open and close. She sank down onto the thick blue comforter and drew her legs up under her skirt, hugging her knees in a vain attempt to chase away the chill in her bones.

How could she have been such a fool these last weeks, allowing her thoughts to revolve around Emmet and what their life together might have been like? Living in a world that could never exist.

She'd dwelt so long on her dissatisfaction with her marriage that she'd lost sight of what life would be like without Dexter.

Maybe she would have been happier with Emmet if she'd married him instead of Dexter five years ago, but now everything was changed. Even if Dexter wasn't a Christian, they shared so many memories. And the children. To truly go back in time and marry Emmet would mean Benjy and Margaret wouldn't exist. Oh, likely there'd be other children—hers and Emmet's. But she couldn't imagine life without feisty Benjy and sweet Margaret.

Or Dexter. In spite of the spiritual life she wished they shared, he *had* been good to her and the children, as her father said earlier. She well knew many men did not treat their wives and families with the love which Dexter showered on them. She didn't truly want to give up life with him.

It was all terribly confusing. She couldn't go back. She wouldn't leave her marriage. Her beliefs demanded commitment, even if her heart wavered. But she wasn't happy, and neither was Dexter.

Her father's comments and prayer last week had infuriated her, but he was right, much as she hated to admit it. She had been trying to force God to do things her way.

Exhaustion overwhelmed her, body and spirit. The thought of beginning again was numbing. Five years of living to redo. It was too much. It was impossible.

It was the only way.

She took a deep breath. Before her resolve could melt away, she rested her forehead against the arms crossed over her knees, and with halting words, asked forgiveness, and thanked God for Dexter's faithfulness as a husband and father.

What had happened through the years to destroy her belief that God would win Dexter's heart? She recalled the conviction with which she'd faced her father before they married: "I shall love him into God's kingdom myself, if I must."

How childish! She'd spoken from no experience at all.

Tears heated her eyes. "I only wanted him to love Thee, Lord," she whispered. "Can that be wrong?"

Nothing spoke to her mind or spirit.

Wearily, she changed into her new flannel nightgown with sprigs of violets against a snow white background. The softness was luxurious and comforting, and she crawled between cool, heather-scented sheets eager to sleep and escape the emotions that had racked her throughout the day and evening.

She couldn't escape. Images of the day's events swam through her mind like a play she was forced to watch. Worst was the memory of Dexter's sorrow-filled eyes when he said in a pain-tightened voice, "I only wish that ye could love me just as I am."

She, who had boasted she would love him into God's kingdom, instead made him feel he wasn't loved at all. She shoved her hands into her hair. How had everything gone so wrong?

She sat bolt upright, staring into the darkness. "Just as I am." Her heart beat wildly in her ears.

That was it!

God loved her just as she was, and no amount of faith or good works would make Him love her more. He just loved her. The same as He loved Dexter.

The same as she must love Dexter.

She'd loved him that way in the beginning. When had she put requirements on her love? In her marriage vows she'd promised to love him always, no "if's" or "but's" attached. Somewhere through the years, she'd changed her commitment.

Excitement danced along her nerves. Her mind exploded with the wonder of new possibilities. She laid back on her pillow, drawing the comforter under her chin, barely noticing how cold the satin felt against her skin.

She laughed, feeling suddenly free. When she learned to love Dexter as God loved him, surely God would answer her prayers and draw Dexter to Him! And save their marriage along the way. Not the fact of their marriage, but the essence, the life of it.

Her father had been right about everything. She was the one who had to change.

Frustration shoved at her excitement. She didn't even know how to begin to change!

"Father God," she whispered into the darkness, "I beg of Thee, teach me how to love my husband."

twelve

Carrie awoke the next morning eager to face the day. The excitement of her "discovery" the night before still danced within her. What would the Lord show her about love?

She was relieved to find Dexter beside her. She couldn't recall him coming to bed. Had he stayed up most of the night? At least he'd come home. Of course, he always did. He'd never stayed away all night because he was angry with her.

She began to put up her hair. Hesitated. Pulled out the hairpins, caught the sides above her ears with tortoiseshell combs, and allowed the black waves to fall down the back of her red-plaid flannel day gown. Her fingers rested a moment where her hair waved on her shoulders, and she remembered the way Dexter liked to caress it. Would he notice she was wearing it down today?

As it turned out, they barely spoke that morning. The children had been about during breakfast, and then he left to meet the Browns for the day, as usual, at Von der Ahe's saloon and ball grounds.

First Corinthians thirteen. The words ran like a refrain to a tune through her head most of the day. From the first she'd realized their significance, of course. First Corinthians thirteen, the love chapter. She went about her duties—aired the house, prepared the day's menus and examined the larder in order to make up a marketing list for the hired girl, checked the water vessels about the house and determined which lamp chimneys needed washing—and played with the children, all the while eagerly awaiting the brief afternoon moments when her children collapsed into their naps and she would have time alone to read the precious chapter.

Surely this was an answer to her prayer last night, she thought more than once as the day wore on. What could be more reasonable than to start with the love chapter of the Bible when learning how to love her husband?

Seated in her favorite tapestry-upholstered rocker, her shoes on the low, curving maroon foot rest, she turned the thin pages eagerly, then read the words aloud.

"Though I speak with the tongues of men and of angels, and have not charity, I am become as sounding brass, or a tinkling cymbal.

"And though I have the gift of prophecy, and understand all mysteries, and all knowledge; and though I have all faith, so that I could remove mountains, and have not charity, I am nothing.

"And though I bestow all my goods to feed the poor, and though I give my body to be burned, and have not charity, it profiteth me nothing.

"Charity suffereth long, and is kind; charity envieth not; charity vaunteth not itself, is not puffed up,

"Doth not behave itself unseemly, seeketh not her own, is not easily provoked, thinketh no evil;

"Rejoiceth not in iniquity, but rejoiceth in the truth;

"Beareth all things, believeth all things, hopeth all things, endureth all things.

"Charity never faileth."

She frowned down at the page. She'd been sure the chapter was going to show her how to put love into practice in actions she could begin immediately, but the wording was woefully lacking in specifics.

One thing for certain, she had "suffered long" during the last five years, but not with kindness! She had badgered Dexter with the knowledge of her suffering, blamed him for causing her suffering by his lack of faith.

She scanned the words again. Strange, not one mention of the passionate emotions that tumbled through a person when one fell in love. Of course, the verses applied to love beyond the relationship between a man and a woman. Still. . .

She wanted to get the *feeling* of love for Dexter back. Wasn't it the passion, the desire for the loved one, that made it possible to act in a loving manner? But the words didn't refer to the emotions she wanted to recapture. Instead it spoke of suffering and enduring.

She rested her head against the chair's high back and sighed. Apparently God's idea of love and her idea of love were far apart. Learning how to love in God's manner wasn't going to be easy.

One of the day's rare rays of sunlight slipped into the room, and the canary burst forth in a gay trill. Smiling, she walked to the tall cage, her heart warming at Dexter's gift.

Canaries always reminded her of Emily Dickinson's poem. "Hope is the thing with feathers that perches in the soul. And sings the tune without the words, and never stops—at all."

Like *love*, she thought, *which never fails.*

Well, she wasn't going to stop hoping either, not at all.

She stuck a finger through the bars of the cage, pulled it back out when the canary ignored it. "I think you've just received your name. From now on, you shall be called Hope."

The front door opened and closed sharply. She knew it was Dexter arriving home, and her hand froze on the cage.

She ran the palms of her suddenly sweaty hands over her flannel covered hips and swallowed nervously, her gaze on the betasseled entry between the parlor and hall. What would he say after last night?

He stopped in the doorway, his hands smoothing his wine-red hair, and she realized he'd removed his coat and hat. His gaze tangled with hers and neither of them moved.

There was a cautious look in his eyes. She tried to give him a radiant smile that would put any doubts he had to rest, but she felt her lips tremble and knew her attempt a failure.

"I. . .I hate when we fight." Her voice quivered just above a whisper.

"Me, too."

She watched his gaze searching hers. There was no trace of his usual smile. Weariness lined his face. But it was the hint of fear in his spring-green eyes that caught her heart in a painful grip. Was he truly afraid he'd lost her love, that she wished she'd married Emmet?

One of them had to remove the fence they'd built these last few years, risk the possibility of being hurt by the other. He'd begun, she realized, when he asked last night about Emmet. It was only right she take the next risk.

She crossed the room slowly, barely noticing the canary's song filling the room. By the time she reached Dexter her heart was pounding as quickly as a trotting pony's hoofs during a race. She laid a hand on each side of his face, stood on tip-toe to kiss him lightly. "All day I've wanted to tell you that I'm glad it is you I married, Dexter Riley."

He didn't respond, didn't return her touch, only continued to search her eyes until she wanted to cry out with the fear writhing within her. Was she mistaken? Did he no longer want her love? Would he tell her instead that he wanted one of those ghastly marriages that were nothing but form?

"Are you for bein' sure, girleen?"

It was all she could do to nod in response. Why had she thought for a moment that risking her heart to tear down the fence between them was noble? It was terrifying.

"I'm not likely to change my stripes at my advanced age."

A smile pulled at her lips. He didn't know the power of God's love! But she only said, "Nor I, so you'll not expect me to stop praying for us."

His mustache twitched, and his hands closed about her wrists lightly. "You wouldn't be my own dear colleen if you gave up practicing your faith."

He took a deep breath, and squared his shoulders. Regret shimmered through her when he released her wrists.

"Der Boss has arranged for us to do a post-season tour with the National League pennant winners, the Detroit Wolverines; a seventeen day tour of the eastern states with a special train of parlor cars. A fifteen match game World's Series, beginning here in St. Louis. What do you think of that?"

Seventeen days! Carrie tried to match Dexter's smile, but knew she was failing miserably. "Quite an honor."

"Have to admit, I'm excited about it. Just hope we play well enough that Der Boss doesn't make us pay our own way home after the last match, like the Chicago's National League owner did to his club last year."

"I doubt Mr. Von der Ahe will be tempted to do that, considering how well the Browns are playing this season."

He started to reach for her. Hesitated. Then circled her waist with his arms. Something in her chest which had been frozen for a long time came to life with a sudden throbbing ache, like fingers frozen by winter wind responding to the warmth of a parlor stove. How long had it been since they'd reached for each other with that precious lack of self-consciousness they'd once known, reached for each other expecting their touch to be welcomed?

"Will you come on the tour?" His voice was rough, his eyes questioning. "There's never been anything like it in Base Ball. I'd like ye with me."

"There's so much going on at church, I'm not sure I can be spared."

The light in his eyes died.

"Perhaps I could get away for a couple days." She didn't want to disappoint him, not now when she believed God wished to give them a new beginning. She'd refused to go the last time he asked her to accompany him on a Base Ball trip, two years ago. "But seventeen days is a long time. Besides, you know Mr. Von der Ahe doesn't approve of the wives traveling with the club."

He nuzzled her neck, his mustache and warm lips sending delightful shivers through her. "Well, I approve, and if Der Boss thinks about it, he will, too. After all, why shouldn't a man play better when his wife is watching?"

"Why, indeed?" she murmured, slipping her arms about his

neck to welcome the lips he lowered to her own.

❧

Carrie's glance swept the opulent restaurant, taking in the three enormous crystal chandeliers beneath the domed, pale blue ceiling edged in gold leaf. Light glittered off silver and fine etched crystal on tables throughout the lower level of the huge room. Opposite her and Dexter was a balcony with half-a-dozen secluded dining areas, each with a table set between sapphire-blue velvet draperies tied back with gold braid from which hung foot-long tassels.

Their own table was in just such a spot on a matching balcony. The orchestra at one end of the room provided a lovely undercurrent of music to the guests' conversations.

"It's beautiful, Dexter."

He beamed at her across the small table. "Best place in Detroit."

"Will Mr. Von der Ahe be upset that you're out tonight? You do play tomorrow."

"I expect Der Boss will save his fury for the base ballers hitting the city's saloons, not those enjoying quiet dinners with their wives."

"I hope you are right. He is awfully unpredictable."

"You said something there!"

"Hey, Riley!"

Guests gasped, then twittered at the loud call. She saw impatience flicker over Dexter's face before following his glance to the lower level to discern the source of the yell. A tall man in an ill-fitting cut-a-way jacket with a top hat sliding off his thick, wavy hair stood grinning up at them.

"Why, it's Tony Mullane!"

"Why did he have to show up here?"

She giggled at Dexter's growl. "I can't believe he'd enter this restaurant, as closely as he holds onto his money." *Except what he spends on drinking*, she amended silently.

Tony was already hurrying up the wide marble stairway at one end of the room, his hand tucked beneath the elbow of a lovely young woman in a low-cut red gown. Without asking whether they were welcome, he seated the woman and himself at their table, his well-cut but thread-bare jacket looking grotesquely out of place against the elegance of white-on-white satin and velvet upholstery.

Uneasiness rippled through her. Even though it was early, the yeasty smell of beer overpowered Tony's cologne.

He didn't bother to introduce his friend. Carrie gave her a friendly smile, while the men greeted each other.

"Who's goin' ta see the rest of the Browns get ta their beds instead of the local jail, with you out bein' respectable with yer wife?"

"They'll have to look out for themselves for once. What are you doing in this part of the country, Mullane?"

Tony leaned back and stuck one of his fat cigars in the corner of his mouth. "Came ta see ya play in the World's Series." He leaned forward, his elbow knocking over an empty crystal wine glass. "Say, I hear Der Boss is gettin' stingy as usual, threatenin' ta give each of you players only a hundred-dollar bonus and keep the club's share of the Series' pot. Pot will probably be 'bout twelve thousand dollars. Any truth ta the rumor?"

"Who knows? Anything is possible when it comes to a club owner and money."

"Heard some other things, too. Like, Comiskey is so mad he's tryin' ta talk some of the other club members into helpin' him throw the Series so's Der Boss won't make as much money."

"You've been around the game a long time, Mullane. Think a base baller's apt to go about talking of throwing a match? Same as cutting off your career."

"Maybe. Have ta be proved first, though. Think you're goin' ta take the Wolverines?"

Dexter shrugged. "We'll try. Your club might have had a chance at this series if you hadn't been suspended again this year."

"Aw, it was only a month or so this time."

"But a bit more serious than usual."

Carrie was surprised to see color steal up from Tony's black and gray striped four-in-hand and creep over his face. Could this be Tony Mullane, embarrassed?

"Guess I had a bit too much ta drink."

"I guess," Dexter repeated dryly. "You threatened to shoot a man, Tony. You need to get yourself in hand and quit rushing the growler."

"Yeah, maybe I will one of these days."

"Do it soon, friend."

She glanced at Tony. He was staring at Dexter, shock written clearly from his famous wavy hairline to his cleft chin, and no wonder. Dexter seldom reprimanded his friends.

Tony shifted his gaze, and his attention quickened. "Hey, look! There's Der Boss!"

He was right. Von der Ahe's distinctive portly shape was indeed in the process of being seated on the balcony across the way. Accompanying him was a woman with an hour-glass figure, her elegant gown weighed down with pearls, her shoulders bare. The purple plume on her hat wrapped almost all the way around the crown above a flattering wide brim.

Carrie's fingers flew to her throat. "Why, that's not Mrs. Von der Ahe!"

Mullane chuckled. "Fortunately for him!"

She'd never seen Dexter's eyes so dark with fury, his full mouth so rigid beneath his mustache. "Mullane, I hate to sound like I'm giving a friend the brush off, but I promised me wife this would be our special night. Ye understand, I'm sure."

Tony weaved a little as he stood. "Sure, I understand." But Carrie noted his thick black brows scrunched together when he looked at his friend. "C'mon, toots, let's leave the man with his wife."

"Does Mr. Von der Ahe often escort women other than his wife when you're out of town with the club?" she asked when Tony and his companion had departed.

He rubbed a large knuckle over his chin and looked out at the crowded room. "I should never have asked you to come on this trip."

"Because I might see him with this. . .this woman?"

He nodded.

"And the other players? Do they—"

"Some of them. They aren't angels. You know that. You've reminded me of it often enough."

"But. . .adultery!"

She should have suspected, of course. She was well aware that women eagerly sought the base ballists' attentions. But to think the club owner, a man well-respected across the country, would be so immoral as to brazenly appear with another woman in one of Detroit's finest restaurants! Why, he didn't even attempt to keep his affair hidden.

And her husband worked for this immoral man!

Grant had warned her before their marriage of the temptations surrounding a base ballist. She remembered thinking Dexter too fine and strong to give into them. Her gaze studied Dexter now with new eyes. Could any man resist temptation when it surrounded him continually?

His touch, covering her hand with his, brought her from her jumbled thoughts. "I've never been unfaithful to ye."

"I know." Could he hear her whispered answer to his fierce declaration?

She believed him—but had she been unfaithful to him?

She'd prayed so stalwartly through the years for him to believe in Christ. She'd hardly thought to ask God to help him stand against temptation in his work each day. *Lord, show me how to pray for him. Show me his needs.*

❧

Waiting in their hotel room the following evening for Dexter to return from the match, she recalled Mullane's accusation of match throwing. She wouldn't have considered it possible the Browns had done such a thing, if it weren't for his suggestion. But what else could she think when the clubs were tied today one-all in the bottom of the thirteenth inning, and then Comiskey—who never failed the club at a critical moment—muffed a throw, allowing the Wolverines to score the winning run?

The door opened, and Dexter entered. He dropped his bowler on a near-by table, then leaned back against the door and stared across the room at her with dull eyes.

She stood, returning his gaze. "Did they lose intentionally?"

He shook his head, weariness in every plane of his face. "I don't know. If so, they didn't ask me to join them in the attempt. They know I'd never do it. I can't believe they'd play it out to thirteen innings and then throw it all away, but. . ."

But Mullane had said it was Comiskey who was instigating the idea, and it was Comiskey who had dropped the ball and lost the match, putting the Browns behind in the Series two games to one.

All last night and today, anger had burned inside her. How could Dexter stand to be a part of this BaseBall world, with its lack of values and morals? How could he work and laugh and play with men who cheated their employer of his money, who cheated themselves of their reputations, who were known even within the base ball community for their unsportsmanlike play, who went so far as to commit adultery, flaunt it, and not be shamed by the fact?

It took all her self-control to keep her tongue and not rail at him as she wished to do, challenging him with the very questions which plagued her. Despair wove through her, shoving away the anger. How could she expect him to walk away from it all when he didn't follow the Lord?

His values were high compared to his fellow base ballers. She knew it, his club mates knew it, and the kranks knew it. It was hard for him to see his friends throwing away their lives on excessive drinking and unfair play and. . .adultery.

Charity "beareth all things, believeth all things, hopeth all things, endureth all things."

She crossed the room and put her arms around him. "*You* played well today, anyway. I'm proud of you."

He rubbed his chin against her hair and sighed with a weariness that caught her in its wave. "Every one of those men has talent and abilities for which other men would exchange fortunes. Why do they continue to live as though life demanded no payment for such foolishness?"

When would he learn, she wondered, *that they would continue to live in that manner until they turned to God?*

thirteen

Delicate, rose-bedecked tea cups clattered cheerfully against matching saucers in the Riley parlor a few weeks later. Carrie's women's Bible-study group filled the room with their chatter and laughter. Now that the day's discussion was behind them, the women were enjoying the petite frosted cakes decorated with sugar-created pansies which Cook had prepared.

A young woman across the room caught her gaze and smiled engagingly. "I'm so glad you suggested a study on First Corinthians thirteen. It's the most wonderful study we've done."

A number of other women nodded or agreed audibly.

"I'm glad you're finding it enlightening."

A chorus of "Oh, my yes!" and "Definitely so!" greeted her.

She darted a look to the other end of the room, where Hannah Kratz sat quietly on the long velvet-covered sofa, and the older woman sent back a sweet, understanding smile. Mrs. Kratz was the only woman here to whom she had confided her reason for wishing to study the chapter.

It was hard to imagine she'd ever been uncomfortable around Hannah, her fellow "church widow." They'd become close friends the last couple years, praying together for their husbands, children, and marriages.

A door slammed, and boys' voices, high pitched with excitement, came from the kitchen. *Dexter must have allowed them in for water once again*, Carrie thought.

Another door slammed, louder this time, and she stood hastily, ready to face the culprit. She'd only taken a step before Dexter burst into the room.

Dread shot through her at the strained look in his eyes. "There's a fire at Sportsman's Park! I'll catch a trolley there.

I'm not knowing when I'll be back!"

He was out of the parlor before he finished speaking.

His interruption had stopped the women's chatter. Only the canary's quivering song broke the silence. Then everyone began speaking at once: how bad was the fire? How had Dexter found out about it?

Their questions went unanswered that evening. It was three in the morning before he returned. Carrie hugged him tightly, heedless of whether her blue satin wrapper was ruined by his soot-covered, water-soaked clothes. The acrid smell of smoke was thick about him, and filled her lungs. Her throat hurt with aching gratitude that he'd not been injured.

"I was so worried!" she whispered into his neck, clinging to him.

When she'd satisfied herself he was truly unhurt, she drew him into the kitchen where his filthy clothing wouldn't harm the furnishings. He sank wearily onto a hard oak chair beside the rectangular work table while she poured a cup of coffee she'd kept heated for him.

He wrapped his hands around the cup and took a large swallow. "Tastes good."

"Was anyone injured?"

He shook his head. His face looked heavy with fatigue. Light from the plain electric ceiling fixture cast eerie shadows over his blackened skin. "No one was hurt, but the players' dressing room was destroyed, and the handball court and gymnasium damaged. So were the clubhouse and Der Boss's Golden Lion Saloon."

"The bleachers?"

"Saved." He set the cup on the table, closed his eyes and slid down, stretching out his legs and resting his head against the hard chair back. "Reporters were there, asking disgusting questions, making slanderous accusations."

"About what?"

"Some of them suggested Der Boss might have started the fire to collect insurance money."

"He wouldn't!" She frowned. "Would he?"

"He's not the city's most honorable man, but I doubt he'd commit arson and robbery."

"My first reaction was the same as yours. But wouldn't a man be capable of almost anything if he practices a. . .adultery?" She found the nasty word difficult to pronounce.

"Because a man condones one sin doesn't mean he condones another," Dexter said impatiently.

"You needn't snap at me! I'm not accused of either sin!"

He caught her hands. "Sorry. I'm just tired."

So was she. She'd been up for hours, worrying about him, praying for him.

"Caruthers was there," he commented.

"Bob Caruthers, the Browns' hurler?"

"Yep. Says Der Boss sold him to Brooklyn for eighty-five hundred dollars."

"But he's the best hurler in the country! Well, one of the best."

He grinned at her, raising his eyebrows in the playful way of old. "So you've been keeping up with Base Ball news, girleen! You'll be a true fanatic yet." The laughter in his eyes slowly died. "Der Boss told Caruthers he's selling other players off, too; four more of our best. If he goes through with it, he'll gut the club."

"Why would Mr. Von der Ahe do that?"

"Says it's because he thinks we lost the World's Series to spite him." He snorted. "The sell-off idea seemed a lot more amusing last year when it was the Chicago owner selling off his base ballers because our team beat them in the World's Series."

"You don't believe that's Mr. Von der Ahe's real reason?"

"Well, rumor is, he needs money."

"Does he?"

His shoulders lifted wearily. "Who knows? Reporters are saying so."

"You mean, they're saying he's selling the base ballers and burning the buildings because he's broke."

"That's the general idea."

"If that's so, why didn't he keep the gate receipts from the World's Series?"

"Guess people have forgotten about that." He sighed, and the depth of it tore at her heart. She lowered herself to his lap and snuggled her cheek against his shoulder, wrinkling her nose at the smell of smoke. His arms slipped around her.

"Didn't think life in Base Ball could get much better than last year and this," he continued. "We won ninety-three matches last year and then won the Series. This year we won ninety-five match games. We were on top of the world until the World's Series. Every man and boy in the country wanted to be one of the St. Louis Browns nines—except those other base ballers who wanted to knock us down a notch," he admitted with a grin. His grin faded. "So why has everything gone so wrong the last few weeks?"

"Everything always goes wrong when people worship themselves and money instead of God."

"God! He's your answer for everything."

She felt him tense, and tried to keep her voice reasonable. "Look at the way most of the base ballers on your club live. They flaunt their sin as if it were a reward instead of something shameful. For instance, that new young hurler, Silver King. Why, you told me yourself that Mr. Von der Ahe kept a woman from prosecuting Mr. King over two illegitimate children, and Mr. King is only nineteen years old! Almost all of the men drink to excess, and make complete fools of themselves in public. Your own good friend, Mr. Browning, is publicly known as Red Light District Distillery Browning. Some of the other base ballers' wives have told me of a number of players who have contracted diseases from. . .loose women. You see, I asked some questions after our Detroit trip. And—"

"I'm not wanting to discuss it."

"Look at your own good friend, Tony Mullane and all the trouble he's been in over the last few years. It's only by God's grace he hasn't been arrested for attempted murder! And Mr. Browning—"

He jerked to his feet, his eyes like black caves as he stared down at her, his voice tight with fury. "Base ballers don't pretend to be angels. But if I remember correctly from me church goin' days, Christians aren't to be judgin', they're to be lovin'. And more to the issue, bad things happen to people who say they serve God, too. Or aren't ye knowing any Christians who lose their jobs, or have fires destroy their business places?"

The truth of his words lanced to her very soul, shaming her. "I'm sorry, I—"

He waved his hands at her in disgust, his lips twisted with contempt. "I'm goin' to bed."

When he had left the room, his back stiff, she dropped into the chair he'd vacated and pressed the palms of her hands over her eyes, which felt gritty and swollen from lack of sleep.

Things had been so wonderful between her and Dexter lately. Had she ruined everything with her accusations?

He must hurt unbearably tonight at the thought of his friends being sold to other clubs, Mr. Von der Ahe pushing their lives in directions they might not wish. Dexter would miss them, regardless of their weaknesses. He'd tried to tell her before of the joy he felt when they played together, working as one—some of the best men in the world at what they did—combining their efforts to give memories that lived for years to the crowds that thrilled to the matches.

He hadn't needed to be reminded of his friends' faults, she knew. He had too often rescued them from the consequences of those faults. He'd bailed some of them out of jail when drunk, lent them money to pay fines, brought them home to keep them from winding up in the "paddy wagon," nursed them, cleaned up after them.

No, he hadn't needed her self-righteous listing of their faults.

He'd needed her comfort. She'd failed him again, even after weeks of studying and praying over the love chapter. "I obviously haven't yet developed that part of love that 'is not puffed up,' Lord!" Indeed, all she'd learned was her inability to love like Christ.

Would she ever discover how to love her husband the way she should? "For Dexter's sake, help me, Lord."

Dexter undressed by the light of the moonbeams shining between the ice-blue draperies, which looked black silhouetted against the windows. He tossed his smoke-clogged clothes in the general direction of a chair with a needleworked pad, and slid between the heather-scented sheets, shivering at their unwarmed smoothness.

Every muscle in his body screamed for sleep, but the anger in his brain wouldn't let rest's healing power come.

God again! Carrie's reverence for God was once one of the things he'd loved about her. Now it was like a weapon she used against him, against their marriage.

Guilt immediately took a punch at his conscience. She didn't mean to use her faith that way, but that was how it affected him. He was tired of getting angry at her and God—all over Someone he didn't believe existed.

He snorted and flopped over on his stomach, punching his pillow into a tight little wad. How dumb could a man be, getting angry at Someone he didn't believe was real?

Was she right about God punishing the Browns for their blatantly immoral acts? But everyone had faults, didn't they? The base ballers just didn't try to hide theirs behind smug, church-going manners.

He wished he could believe in God. Not that he saw any benefit in being a believer, except that he wouldn't be fighting with Carrie as much. He didn't expect God would bother to repair Von der Ahe's Sportsman's Park, or buy back Bob Caruthers' contract and let the Browns stay one big happy family. Never did see God going out of His way for any of the people He was supposed to love so much.

'Course, if all faith in God did was make Carrie love him more, it would be well worth any bother it caused. He had promised before they married that he'd attend church and give God a try. A bit of guilt wriggled through him. He hadn't given Him much of a try, but then, God being God, He shouldn't need too much time to prove Himself, should He?

He rolled onto his back again, pressing the heels of his hands to his eyes. He had to get some sleep. First day of his off-season law clerk position started tomorrow. Today, that is, in just a couple hours.

He hated arguing with Carrie. He could count on not sleeping well after a quarrel, at least until they resolved things. Trouble was, the arguments about God were never resolved.

He threw his hands in the air and let them drop with a soft "thud" on the thick bed covers. "I give up! If Ye're there, God—and I'm not sayin' Ye are, mind Ye—but if Ye are, would Ye be findin' a way to show me? For Carrie's sake."

He turned onto his side. *Thought people were supposed to feel better when they prayed.* He didn't. He *sure* didn't.

"If Ye happen to be answerin' prayers tonight, I could be usin' some sleep."

Well, it couldn't hurt to ask.

fourteen

1888

Carrie glanced up from the pile of silver she was polishing when Dexter entered the kitchen. Early summer sunlight streamed through the windows between sheer yellow curtains. She noticed with a sudden realization of passing time how the cheerful rays intensified the green of his eyes, and highlighted the grooves bracketing his mouth which had deepened in the six years since they'd met.

He leaned a hip against the wooden table beside the sink, tossing a base ball casually with one hand in the habit Benjy and Joey had adopted. "The lads play their first match against the West Side club tomorrow afternoon. Will you come?"

"Child base ballers have kranks and kranklets now, too?" Carrie wiped her hands down her practical, oversized navy-and-green-striped apron, stalling for time. She hated always disappointing him when he asked her to do things, but her commitments at the church filled most of her afternoons and evenings. And with the spring cleaning so far behind due to the rain that fell almost the entire month of May—

"Say you'll come, Carrie. The lads want you to see their new ball grounds."

"I don't know whether I can spare the time." She waved a hand toward the sink filled with recently polished silver. "There's the spring cleaning to be completed, and it's already June, and—"

"Isn't that what we're paying Hannah's girl, Millie, to do so you and Jane can keep up with your own duties?"

"Now if that isn't just like a man! You have no idea how much is involved in keeping a house respectably clean. Millie cannot possibly do the entire spring cleaning for a home this size herself."

"Well, it won't hurt for the two of you to fall one afternoon behind."

"We're already a month behind! All the woolen garments, rugs, and blankets must be snapped, brushed, and packed in moth protectors and wrappers. The wicker and wooden porch furniture has still not been painted for summer—and you know we'll need that for the next meeting of the Ladies' Needlework Society if it doesn't rain. Every wall in the house must be dusted, all the chimneys and shades from the chandeliers and gas jets cleaned, the windows washed, the door handles polished, the dining room and parlor cleaned, and—"

She stopped for a breath and he took advantage to interrupt. "My apologies for misunderstanding the gravity of the situation. Perhaps I shouldn't have had this house built for us, and caused you all this trouble."

"I love this house!" she responded to his teasing words, "but it does require much upkeep. Without Cook, Jane, and Millie, I couldn't possibly run it." She leaned toward him and shared in a conspiratorial whisper, "To be honest, when the help was first hired, I was almost afraid to speak to you for fear something personal in nature might be overheard."

His whoop of laughter lightened her spirits. It had been a long time since they'd truly laughed together. "I felt the same way."

She spread her hands. "As you can see, there is much to be done. And I've Bible study tomorrow."

"Is it to be held here again?"

Was he upset over the meetings she held in their home? If so, neither his voice or manner revealed it. "No, it will be at Mother's. Hannah was supposed to hostess it, but her husband isn't feeling well."

"Touch of the grippe, I suppose. With the cold rains we've had lately, it's pretty common."

"I'm surprised Joey and Benjy haven't come down with it. The rain hasn't kept them from practicing Base Ball, in spite of my protests. The other day during that bad storm I had to resort to hiding the new bat you had made for Benjy to keep him from going out to play."

Dexter braced a hip against the iron sink, tossed the ball, and grinned. "He's just a base baller, born and bred."

"If he's born to it, why does he have to practice so much?"

"I did the same thing when I was a lad. Never could stand to let a day go by without seeing whether I'd improved from the day before."

She leaned against the counter beside him, loving the thought of him at Benjy's age. "I wish I'd known you as a boy."

"No you don't. Girls and boys are mortal enemies at that age." He wiggled his eyebrows. "I think we like each other much better now than we would have then."

"Oh, pooh!" She turned away from him and went back to work on the silver. "Joey's been awfully good with Benjy, hasn't he? He plays so patiently with him, instead of teasing him unmercifully the way boys can do with one a couple years younger."

"Teaching him great things, too. Like where to find the fattest nightcrawlers for fishing."

"Wonderful knowledge, I must admit."

He chuckled at her sarcasm.

"I have been concerned for the boy lately, Dexter. Remember saying last year that Joey seemed spindly for his age? Benjy is much rounder and healthier."

"Joey's not holding his own against the rest of the lads on the club, either. Maybe he's just one of those natural beanpoles."

"Maybe." She could see by his frown he didn't believe it.

"Enough of this stalling, woman. Will you come tomorrow or not?"

It must be especially important to him; he doesn't usually press me like this, even couching it in that pretend gruff voice.

She made a saucy face. "Since you want me so awfully, I suppose I've no choice but to join you."

He dropped a quick kiss on the bridge of her nose. "Good! It will make the lads' day."

Maybe, she thought, watching him leave the room, *but I already feel guilty for missing Bible study.* Perhaps she should ask her father at the mid-week service tonight whether she'd done the right thing.

❧

"Of course you did the right thing," Rev. Chambers declared unequivocally while she helped him straighten up the pews after the service, putting hymnals and Bibles in their proper places. "Don't know why God wouldn't want you to join your husband and children in a bit of pleasure."

"I know He wouldn't deny me their company. It's just. . .well, I want so desperately for Dexter to become a believer. . .and you know what it says in First Peter about a wife winning her husband to the Lord by her example."

He stroked his trim black and gray beard with long fingers. "First Peter. Hmmm. Are you referring to the third chapter, where it says 'Likewise, ye wives, be in subjection to your own husbands that, if any obey not the word, they also may without the word be won by the conversation of the wives; while they behold your chaste conversation coupled with fear'?"

"Yes, that's it. I haven't succeeded in winning him with my nagging, so I hoped my example would do so."

"By attending church functions?"

"Partly, yes."

"Have you forgotten the first part of the verse?"

"What do you mean?"

"The part that says, 'be in subjection to your own husbands.'"

"Oh." She shifted uncomfortably. She didn't like to think about that part.

"A few verses further along Peter reminds the reader of Sarah. Do you recall how she obeyed her husband, Abraham, when they were in Egypt?"

Uncomfortable warmth spread up her neck and over her face. "Yes. Abraham told her to let Pharaoh think she was his unmarried sister, and allow him to take her into his home, so his own life wouldn't be endangered."

"That's right, and God protected her there. I doubt Dexter will expect anything of you like Abraham asked of Sarah. I can hardly see why the Lord will be upset with either of you for watching some boys play Base Ball." He peered at her over the top of his spectacles. "It's not the most respectable pastime, but the boys won't be playing Sunday ball or serving beer, I presume, like the Browns do at Statesman's Park."

She smiled briefly, then sobered. "But, what if Dexter expects me to give up more of my church activities?"

"Has he asked you to do so?"

"No, never."

"What if he does? Think you'll lose your faith?"

"Of course not, but—"

"Think the church can't get along without your hand in every organization?"

"No! And I'm not in every organization!"

He stroked his beard again, pursed his lips. "Nope. Haven't seen you at the men's Bible studies. Not yet, anyway."

"Father!"

He patted her shoulder. "Now don't be getting into a tizzy over nothing. You've been a faithful member of this congregation. I've appreciated your efforts, and I'm certain the rest of the members have, too. But as the Good Book says, there's a time for every season under heaven, and this just might be your season to be a Sarah. Besides, won't hurt some of the other women in the church to fill in where you've been working so hard."

"But, Mother was always helping at the church or assisting one of the members when we were growing up. She still does so."

"Your mother married a minister. You married a base ballist. He has different needs from his wife than a minister."

She'd have to reflect on that. Surely he couldn't mean the Lord meant for her to assist Dexter playing ball! "What if you can't find anyone to replace me?"

"People are always replaceable. One of the facts of life."

He makes it sound as if I won't even be missed. He'll change his mind if I do give up some of my commitments, and he finds how difficult it can be to convince people to help. "Well, if you're certain it's what I should do—"

At his impatient nod, she walked toward the back of the church. *My chin is probably dragging worse than the train on my dress.* She loved her church work and being with others who loved the Lord. She wasn't looking forward a bit to the possibility of a "Sarah's Season."

"Oh, Carrie!"

She spun around. "Yes?"

"You'll not give up the children's Sunday school, I hope?"

"Not if you'd rather I didn't, unless Dexter specifically asks it of me." Joy bubbled up inside. There was nothing she enjoyed more than working with the children, and she couldn't imagine Dexter asking her to relinquish it.

❧

The sun blazed from a cloudless sky late the next afternoon when they arrived at the lot two blocks from their home where the match game was to be held. Joey and Benjy, who had accompanied them, rushed to join the boys already busy "warming up," as they called their practice. Millie and Jane were watching over Margaret.

Carrie tucked a hand in Dexter's elbow. "Benjy must have asked fifty times today whether it wasn't time for the match to begin. He's been on pins and needles! I must admit, I've caught a bit of his excitement."

He smiled down into her face, creating a world with just the two of them, in spite of the two dozen boys hollering only a few yards away. The smile warmed the green of his eyes, wrapped around her heart, and put to rest the guilt which had been festering in her conscience like a splinter over the time she'd stolen to join them.

She unfolded the brown wool blanket she'd brought to sit upon. Before it touched the ground, Benjy was running toward her. "Hey, what do you think you're doing, Mom? You have to sit on the bleachers, you know!"

"Bleachers?"

He grabbed her hand and tugged. "Yes, over there." He nodded to the other side of the lot, where a warped, weathered board lay across two overturned fruit boxes in the midst of calf-high weeds. "We built it 'specially for you."

She shared an amused glance with Dexter, who was losing a valiant struggle not to laugh. He grabbed the unfurled blanket and started across the lot behind them. She smiled her thanks when he laid the blanket across the dirty old board.

Benjy held her hand in a most gentlemanly manner, his five-year-old chest puffed out with importance, when she lowered herself with as much grace as possible to her wobbly seat of honor. In a flash, he rejoined his friends.

Trying not to think of the bugs and wood ticks in the weeds about her long skirt and high-topped shoes, she looked out at the field, and was surprised to find the boys had stopped practicing to watch her be seated.

Dexter set down a large tin pail with a dipper hooked over the edge. "The lads will be glad you thought to bring this water along."

From the bench beside her she lifted a large linen dishtowel tied in a knot. "I expect they'll enjoy the sugar cookies, too."

He rested a foot on the board, leaned an elbow on his knee, glanced at the boys, then back at her. "Feel like a queen?"

"Indeed I do."

"Consider me your servant, also, m'lady."

She laughed at his nonsense. It had been the right thing to do, sharing this day with him. This time, anyway.

"I understand why Der Boss calls the Browns 'mein poys' after working with these youngsters. The lads out there may be just a bunch of ragtag kids who won't even remember me in a few years, but to me they're 'me boys.'"

His husky declaration brought a lump to her throat. She wanted to hug him for his uncharacteristically sweet admission, but restrained herself. She was sure 'his laddies' wouldn't approve of such female behavior bestowed upon their "Cap," as they called him, short for "captain."

The last couple days of sunny weather had begun to dry the water-soaked ground, but there were still puddles here and there on the weedy, unleveled lot. She noticed with dismay that a number of the boys' trousers were already mud-covered, and was grateful she had someone to help with the wash. Many of the boys' mothers hadn't that luxury, and a couple, she knew, took in other people's wash.

At least all those flying little feet wouldn't be tracking mud across her kitchen floor today! She turned to Dexter. "Did I remember to thank you for purchasing this lot for the boys? Millie and Jane thank you, too!"

"So do our neighbors and my pocketbook, after the glass I've replaced over the last couple years."

He called the boys over and opened the leather valise he'd brought, pulling out a dozen black and white striped jockey hats. "Thought you lads should look like a ball club."

Cries of pleasure rewarded "Cap."

"Maybe we can all wear black socks in the next match, too, like real base ballers," Joey offered eagerly. The other boys jumped on the idea.

When the game began, Carrie was joined by a number of the players' sisters and brothers, but no other mothers. Guilt slipped its wedge into her conscience again at the thought that the other mothers were working, not watching boys play.

With an effort, she pictured herself shoving the guilt out the door of her mind, and hanging out a plaque emblazoned with the words Sarah's Season. Silly, perhaps, but it helped.

She enjoyed cheering the boys on, along with the help of the young kranks and kranklets.

As Dexter had said, it was rather a ragtag group. The boys ranged in age roughly from seven to ten, with only a couple as young as Benjy. She was surprised to see how well he performed in comparison to the older boys. But then, she reminded herself, he was Dexter's son.

It was Joey's play that signaled alarm within her. He was the worst player on the field. He hadn't the strength or the dexterity of the other boys. Even Benjy was more coordinated in his efforts. No wonder Dexter had expressed concern.

Her heart went out to the gangly boy in the third inning when there were three boys on base and it was Joey's turn as batsman. Some of the older boys pleaded with Dexter to let someone else bat.

Joey lowered the willow until the large end rested on the weed-covered ground, and turned large eyes on Dexter, awaiting his verdict.

Dexter, arms crossed over his wide chest, nodded at him calmly. "Go ahead, Joey. Do your best."

As Joey stepped up to the dirt-filled flour sack that served as home base, Dexter turned to the rest of the club. Carrie couldn't recall ever seeing his face set so sternly. "A club *always* supports its mates."

The words were spoken low and quietly, but the effect was instantaneous. There were no more groans or comments, although glaring eyes and pouting lips filled the young faces.

Everyone was surprised when Joey's third wobbly strike at the ball connected with just enough force to knock it half-way to the hurler. The runner on third made it to home base only inches before the ball. The Rangers went wild.

Joey's next turn as batsman wasn't as successful. Or his next. He struck out both times. His clubmates forgot their earlier cheers for the run he'd batted in, though Dexter's sharp looks reminded them to hold their ridicule in check.

She'd been so jealous of the time Dexter spent with the Rangers that she hadn't realized how much he loved the boys. Did he lavish so much attention on them because he wanted them to know the approval he hadn't known as a child? Was that why it was so important to him that the boys learn to be loyal to their clubmates, so that at least within the Rangers, they would always know they were accepted?

The thought brought her up short, forcing her attention from the boys in front of her to the boy her husband had been. Her gaze rested on him, trying to imagine him a self-conscious boy with wavy dark hair and shining green eyes and skinned knees. Did part of him still need that respect he'd been denied by the church members he'd known as a child? Was it that insecure little boy he'd once been who was behind the statement on their fifth anniversary last fall, his statement that he wished she could love him, just as he was?

A ball whizzing past her head jolted her back to the present. A moment later she was cheering the Ranger running around the bases as fast as his short legs would carry him, weeds whipping as he raced past.

She was as thrilled when the Rangers won as she'd been the first time she watched Dexter's club win on a day in May six years ago. From the sparkle in Dexter's eyes and the bounce in his walk, she suspected he felt the same.

He caught her hand in his while walking home. For over a year he had stopped reaching for her in those simple, almost unconscious ways that show a man cares for a woman and is glad to have her beside him. At his touch, her eyes heated with threatening tears and her throat constricted.

Perhaps this Sarah's Season wouldn't be so intolerable after all.

fifteen

September, 1889

Sun-drenched color from the tall stained-glass windows set in gray limestone walls dappled the chapel. The air was thick with the scent of delicate white, yellow, and pink rosebuds on the edge of opening to life—like Rose Marie, the little girl in Grant's arms.

Carrie watched Phoebe straightened a fold of Rose Marie's French Nainsook gown, which fell at least two feet beyond the six-week-old child's toes. Tiny embroidery covered the last six inches of the robe.

Grant's gaze met Phoebe's above the child's head, and Carrie's throat constricted at the love that passed between them. What a special day for them!

A couple she didn't know—friends of Phoebe's—stood before the altar and her father with Grant and Phoebe. Strange to think her brother and his wife had chosen someone other than her and Dexter to raise Rose Marie should anything happen to them.

Perhaps it wasn't strange. Why would they want her and Dexter to raise their child? She had chosen to marry a man who didn't serve the Lord. Amazing, the consequences one never realizes will result from one's actions. She never thought before that her brother wouldn't trust her with his children.

If she'd married Emmet, her brother and Phoebe would be willing to entrust Rose Marie to her.

It was a short but heart-tugging ceremony dedicating Rose Marie to the Lord. Prayers were offered by not only her father, but also Grant and Phoebe.

What would it be like to pray together with Dexter over their children, she wondered, listening to Grant's simple prayer. The thought left an aching void of loneliness in her chest. If she had married Emmet—

I didn't. I won't allow myself to dwell on what might have been. Besides, it's not Emmet I miss, but the spiritual closeness he and I would have had that Dexter and I don't share.

Will our children be the worse for our inability to pray for them together, Lord? When they are older, will they choose not to walk with Thee, the way Hannah's children have done, because their father doesn't know Thee? Fear slithered into her heart at the thought. Another consequence she hadn't considered when she agreed to marry Dexter. When she insisted upon marrying him, she corrected herself.

Margaret leaned against her, and she looked down to see her daughter stretching her slender neck above the pew in front of them, her eyes alight with excitement at was happening with her new little cousin.

Beside her, Benjy tried hard not to be impressed, his bottom lip jutting out in a pout, and his arms crossed hard over his two piece suit of checked cassimere, but the green eyes so like his father's showed a glimmer of interest, just the same.

She reached behind Margaret and pulled the black and white Rangers hat from Benjy's head. When and how had he managed to slip that on without her or Dexter seeing it?

His hand whipped to his suddenly bare head. He caught sight of the hat in her hand, and his eyes widened before he deepened his scowl.

On the other side of her, Dexter looked down at the hat, raised his eyebrows, glanced at his son, and grinned. He tucked her gloved hand beneath his elbow. A moment later he nodded toward Grant and Rose Marie, then leaned down with mischief dancing in his eyes to whisper, "Why don't we have another one of those?"

She knew she was blushing all the way from the high ivory lace neck of her new pink chiffon gown to her hairline, though no one else heard him. Even so, she couldn't keep from smiling at his query. He did so love children. It was one of the dear things about the man.

But she wished they could pray together for the children. Or anything else, for that matter.

The thought returned to her later that day while watching Dexter hold little Rose Marie. After the service, the family had come to her and Dexter's home for dinner and visiting. They didn't see nearly enough of Grant and Phoebe, since the couple lived in Ridgeville, where she and Grant had grown up.

When Rose Marie made it obvious she'd had quite enough visiting for the afternoon, Carrie accompanied Grant to Margaret's room. The reluctance with which he gently laid the child in the bonneted cradle from Margaret's baby days caused a sweet twinge in her breast. She blinked back a mist of tears.

"What do you think of your new niece?"

"I think she is far lovelier than a girl should expect to be with you for a father."

He grinned from ear to ear. "I agree completely."

He lightly ran a blunt finger-tip over Rose Marie's round cheek. "I wonder what her life will be like, what kind of man she will marry? I hope he's the best man on the face of the earth."

The fierceness in his voice choked her, and it was a moment before she could say, "Dexter said the same thing when Margaret was born. The two of you might give the girls a chance to grow up before you worry over their marriage partners."

"But it makes so much difference in life, who you choose to spend it with." He looked up, pinning her gaze. "Doesn't it?"

What does he want me to say? That I should have married Emmet instead of Dexter? Or was part of him sorry he hadn't married Amanda? The memory of him and Phoebe at the dedication service flashed in her mind. They appeared devoted to each other, but were they? "It seems almost. . .indecent. . .to ask this, but do you ever," she caught her bottom lip in her teeth, grabbed her courage, and rushed boldly on. "Do you ever miss Amanda? Are you sorry—" she couldn't complete the sentence.

Dusky color flooding his face didn't reassure her. His lips tightened.

"Forgive me for asking." She turned her back to him, unnecessarily rearranging Rose Marie's soft, tiny blanket.

"It's all right, Carrie. Amanda and I, we weren't at the right places in our lives to be together." She pivoted slowly to face him, her gaze searching his eyes, wondering if they hid a private pain. "I finally realized I was trying to push Amanda into becoming a Christian before she was ready."

"But the Bible clearly tells us we're to tell people about Him."

He nodded. "I tried to convince myself that was all I was doing. I wanted her to know Him, but I wasn't willing to wait for Him to water the seeds you and I and others planted in her life. I wanted her to believe when I thought she should, not when God had her heart fully prepared for Him. I didn't help God's efforts. I only hope I didn't hinder them.

"Fond as I was of her, I had no right courting her. I knew how she felt about the Lord from the beginning. It wasn't right, allowing her to think we might have a future together. If I'd cared for her as much as I thought I did, I wouldn't have hurt her."

Was that what she'd been doing with Dexter? Pushing him, expecting him to accept beliefs before God finished the necessary work in his life? It would be like expecting a person barely introduced to the fundamentals of Base Ball to be a hurler for a major league club.

Grant rested a slender hand on her shoulder. A smile tipped his lips. "Don't worry about me, little sister. I love my wife. If I had to make the choice again, I'd choose Phoebe."

"I'm glad. Amanda's beliefs haven't changed."

He grimaced. "I'm sorry to hear that."

"She hasn't married, either." She didn't think he'd wish to be burdened with the knowledge that Amanda still loved him.

"Does she still see Browning?"

"Yes."

"Browning is a confirmed bachelor and a drunkard. He's no good for her." His mouth tightened. "Beats me why some people fight God so hard."

She wondered whether he was referring to Amanda, Mr.

Browning, or both.

She sighed deeply, swallowed her pride, and confided, "Last year I actually hoped Dexter might be changing. He was upset over the way things were going with his friends, their drinking and cheating and such, and with Mr. Von der Ahe selling so many members of the Browns the year before. He and the others were so sure the club's future was destroyed when the five best players were sold. But then—"

"Then the Browns took a group of untested rookies and won the '88 pennant anyway, to the surprise of everyone."

"Yes. I'd hoped he would see that people couldn't turn their backs on God and expect Him to bless them in return, but then everything worked out so well for the Browns. Why did God do that?" Was that her voice, scaling an octave in frustration?

His laugh broke through the strain in the room. "Are you asking why God didn't punish your husband and Von der Ahe?"

"I guess that does sound silly." Her smile felt sheepish.

"A mite. Must have pleased you when the major leagues slapped a $2,500 salary cap on the players, and reduced your husband's earnings."

He chuckled when she wrinkled her nose at him, but then sobered. "Dexter is a fine man. Finer than most. He just doesn't believe in God."

"Yes, but that is a large 'just.'"

How much longer would she have to wait for Dexter to open his heart to the Lord, she wondered, walking beside Grant back to the parlor.

Charity suffereth long. . .endureth all things. She had been looking for things to do, actions she could take, when she first read the love chapter two years ago. Was she being told, instead of doing, to wait and allow God time to work? Was that one of the things God meant for her to do during her Sarah's Season, to cease struggling and wait for Him to act? Could He ask anything more difficult?

Is anything too difficult to endure for Dexter's soul?

The words were spoken only in her heart, but she heard them

as clearly as though they'd been spoken aloud. Of course nothing was too difficult! Did the Bible not say that we can do all things through Christ, who strengtheneth us?

Charity suffereth long. . .beareth all things, believeth all things, hopeth all things, endureth all things. She hadn't realized what a large part of love involved waiting!

"Base Ball is even gaining a bit of respectability now that President Harrison's wife has admitted to enjoying the matches," Dexter was saying when they entered the parlor.

"And how is that boy doing, that Joey you speak of so often?" her father asked when the laughter died down.

Her glance collided with Dexter's. They didn't care to discuss Joey too candidly in front of Benjy. "He's weaker," Dexter replied cautiously. "Can't play with the lads much anymore; it tires him out. But he comes to most of the matches, and gives advice to the little guys, keeps up with the willows, things like that."

Joey had begun getting weaker about six months ago. His spirits were still cheerful—most of the time, anyway, when he wasn't thinking about the Base Ball he was missing.

"He still tags about Dexter every available minute," she shared.

He smiled across the room at her. "That's not entirely accurate. I have to share him with you, like I do most of the lads now." He turned to Grant. "The lads have taken to coming over after every game for her cake and lemonade. She's the Rangers' private nurse; bandages the blackened eyes, split lips, and bunged fingers that happen to base ballers of all ages. They call her Mrs. Cap."

The pride in his voice and eyes filled her with gratitude for the closeness God was slowly working between them. "They ask Dexter's advice on every topic under the sun. You'd think not one of them had parents with whom to consult."

How could she have considered for a moment that she might not love this man? What if she hadn't decided to hang on tight to her vows and work to make their marriage good? Would they still be at each others' throats, living under one roof but a world apart in their hearts?

"Speaking of the Rangers, I've something to show you."

She hurried from the room, returning with a hat box. Opening it, she handed a bib of white flannel to Dexter and another to Benjy. "I've made one for each member of the club."

Dexter's grin couldn't have grown wider. "Shields for the lads' shirts, with a fancy black "R" for Rangers. Well done, girleen o' mine!"

Her parents, Grant and Phoebe, and Phoebe's parents and friends crowded about to see, while Benjy immediately tied his shield over his suit jacket with its wide white collar.

A pounding at the front door broke into the group's admiring comments. A moment later, the maid appeared at Carrie's side, and Carrie hurried into the hall to greet Hannah's daughter, a pale Millie Kratz.

"Oh, Mrs. Riley, come quick! Ma needs you!"

"Has your father taken worse?"

"He's. . .he's dead!"

❧

Was the early September wind unusually chilly? Carrie wondered three days later, shivering on the bleachers close behind the Browns' bench in Brooklyn's Washington Park. The roar of the fifteen thousand spectators and the ever-present smell of cigars and beer on nearby kranks barely touched her awareness today.

The Browns were ahead three to two in the sixth inning, and Comiskey, with one of the sneaky tactics Dexter so deplored, was arguing fiercely with the umpire that it was too dark to continue—much to the kranks' dismay.

She couldn't care less whether the match continued. Dexter had thought it would do her good to get away for a few days following Mr. Kratz's death, and she'd finally agreed to accompany him for the three-match series with the Brooklyn Bridegrooms. It wasn't possible to leave behind her burden for Hannah, however.

Hannah's husband is dead, Lord. How could Thee have allowed him to die before he came to believe in Thee? Didn't

Hannah's years of prayers and faithfulness count for anything in Thy sight? Forty-five years she trusted Thee to save him!

Her heart had been frozen since Millie told of her father's death. Helping Hannah through the last few days was the most difficult thing she'd ever been called upon to do. She could assist her with decisions, with the children, with refreshments for the guests who came to express their sympathy—but she had nothing to share to help her grieving spirit. What could she say when they both knew her husband hadn't believed in God?

She knew well her father's explanation of why people like Mr. Kratz—people with every chance to know the Lord—never came to Him. God wouldn't force Himself on those who don't want Him, he would say. He's given each of us the power to choose whether we will love Him or not. He won't take that away from us. He wouldn't take it away from Mr. Kratz. He wouldn't take it away from Dexter.

And that was the most frightening thought of

But I believed if I loved Dexter the way Thou dost love him, he would come to Thee!

The way God loved him. Unconditionally. Expecting nothing in return. Even Dexter's salvation.

Her heart stumbled.

She'd known, at least in her mind, that it was possible to go through the rest of their lives together loving Dexter and praying for him and still to never see him come to the Lord, but she hadn't truly grasped the possibility. Loving him as she did, she couldn't imagine such a thing. She'd believed Dexter would accept Christ's gift of salvation eventually, even if they were both bent and gray at the time.

But that was what God had meant by loving him the way God loved him. Expect *nothing* back. Only give love.

The spectators about her rose to their feet in a body, their bellow all but lifting the roof which covered the grandstand. It jerked her out of her absorption.

Mr. Von der Ahe was setting candles about the Browns' bench, supporting Charlie Comiskey's contention it was too dark to continue the match.

It wasn't too dark to see a form hurtle through the air and bounce off the ground near the candles. And then another, and another, and then a drove. Some made crashing sounds, and she realized with a coiling of fear in her stomach that outraged kranks were tossing beer steins, attempting to put out the candles, succeeding in knocking some over.

The Browns ducked, attempting to protect themselves with upraised arms from the missiles, stumbling away from the flickering flames which were inciting the crowd.

Her heart pounding in her throat, Carrie's gaze searched for Dexter, but she couldn't see over the wild throng. She stepped up on the bleacher and stretched her neck. Catching sight of him about ten feet from the bench lessened her fear slightly.

"Fire!"

The people almost trampled each other in their attempt to flee the flames which suddenly leaped only a few feet away, licking at the grandstand. Had the overturned candles started the conflagration?

She caught sight of Browns team members darting toward the flames, Dexter among them. They were joined by spectators and players from the Bridegrooms, and the flames were soon thoroughly doused—not so the clubs' or kranks' anger.

Grumbling loudly, the crowd returned to their places. They stood rather than sat, not wanting to miss a moment of passionate disagreement. The clubs' captains and the umpire gave them a show in ungentlemanly behavior, continuing to argue over whether it was too dark to play. The umpire sided with the Bridegrooms, in spite of the overcast skies, and play continued.

Carrie's attention was fully on the match now. Her hands clenched together in her lap until the knuckles ached. Police had arrived and stood along the edge of the grounds. Would Dexter and the others need their protection?

She breathed a prayer of thanksgiving when the ninth inning was reached with the Browns ahead four to two. The match would soon be over, and she and Dexter safely back at their hotel.

Her relief was short-lived. The Bridegrooms were about to come up to bat when the Browns' outfielder was caught dunking the ball in a bucket of water. She thought the crowd would stampede the field in their fury, but with the encouragement of the police, they eventually settled down to watch the finish—although amidst complaints as loud as rumbling thunder.

The rumble grew to a cheer from excited Brooklyn kranks when one of the Bridegrooms attempted to steal second base and arrived at almost the same time as the ball thrown by the Browns' catcher. The runner was declared safe.

The cheer changed back to dangerous thunder when Comiskey insisted the throw beat the man to the base, but the umpire was unable to tell due to darkness.

Carrie hugged her arms to her chest and looked at the furious faces about her—it wasn't too dark to see the kranks' angry expressions. Couldn't Charlie tell by now that the umpire wasn't going to be convinced by his argument of darkness? The Browns were ahead by two runs. Hadn't he enough faith in his clubmates to play the match to the finish? It was that competitive nature that drove him. Win at any price.

Competition. It was built into each of the players so fiercely it was as much a part of them as their fingers or noses or hearts.

She was in a competition, too—a competition for Dexter's soul.

Forgetting the crowd about her, she lifted her face. "Help me, Lord."

Her whisper was lost in the crowd's roar. She realized suddenly that Comiskey had pulled the club off the grounds, and forfeited the match. She glanced at the marquisite watch pinned to her jacket. It was just past six-thirty.

Beer steins hurtled through the air once more, pelting the Browns. The police attempts to protect the players were woefully inadequate.

She pushed through the crowd, her fear for Dexter's soul temporarily routed in the immediate, all-consuming fear for his physical safety.

sixteen

Dexter received only minor bruises and cuts from the rain of beer steins, to Carrie's relief. The player who was caught drenching the ball received the worst of the attack. Still, there were two matches yet to be played against the Brooklyn Bridegrooms, and the attitude of the kranks was frightening.

She felt much better the next day when the Browns forfeited the Sunday match, furious they'd been denied their share of the Saturday gate receipts for withdrawing from the Candlelight Match, as it was being called.

The withholding of the money convinced the club manager, Charlie Comiskey, and Mr. Von der Ahe to play the final match on Tuesday, however. Dexter assured her extra police protection had been arranged for the Browns, but rather than calming her fears, the information established their validity to her.

She was even more upset when Dexter insisted she return by train to St. Louis on Monday, knowing he was trying to keep her from a possibly dangerous situation. The lurid newspaper reports about the Candlelight Match and consequent Browns-Bridegrooms feud which she devoured on the long trip back did nothing to comfort her. She lifted numerous prayers for Dexter's safety and the club's, and she slept little.

Tuesday afternoon she took a covered cab to Frank's Irish Stars Saloon. Since Frank had a telegraph service there in order to draw customers interested in the latest sports news from across the country—as did many other saloons—she knew he would hear immediately if a serious situation developed during the match.

She was so relieved to find the Tuesday game had been postponed due to rain, and no attack made upon the police-protected

Browns by the kranks, that she threw her arms around the bulky Frank and thanked him as though he was personally responsible for the good news.

The deep chuckle so unlike Dexter's laugh shook his large chest when she hastily stepped back. His hands grasped her waist, steadying them both.

"Dexter will be comin' back to ye safe and sound, don't be worrying."

"I hope so." The friendly twinkle in his eyes made her feel welcome in spite of their past animosity.

He waved a large hand at a man behind the counter. "Bring the colleen a cup of coffee."

"Oh, I couldn't! I must be getting home." Now that she knew the situation in Brooklyn, she was eager to leave the saloon with its rough looking characters and yeasty odor.

He brushed away her protest, pulling out a chair at a nearby table. "I want to hear from your own lips what happened at Brooklyn. Did any of those Bridegrooms' kranks' beer steins hit me baby brother?"

She hesitated for a moment, then relented and took the seat he offered her. After all, he loved Dexter, too. Of course he'd want to know what had happened.

In the end, she surprised herself by inviting him, his wife, and Amanda to dinner when Dexter arrived back. It had been years since any of Dexter's family other than Amanda dined with them. She hadn't cared for his brothers' company, and Dexter hadn't insisted, choosing instead to visit his family alone.

It would be good for him to have friendly faces around when he returned from this trip, she told herself, waving good-bye to Frank while he watched the cab he'd paid for pull away from the saloon to take her home.

She put extra care into her toilette the next day. There would be no cheering crowds at the depot today as there had been during the Browns' glory years. Those close to the base ballers would be the only welcoming faces.

Fancy combs with faux pearls held the sides of her hair back from her face in flattering rolls, allowing the back to hang in loose waves the way Dexter liked. The combs would go well with the new gown of swirled rose silk she planned to wear for dinner that evening.

The children grew tired of watching for the horse-drawn cab and were out playing with neighbor children when he arrived at the house.

Carrie was at the door when he reached it. He dropped his valise on the doorstep and wrapped his arms around her, burying his face in her hair. His breath was warm against her neck, and she welcomed the touch of his lips there.

"I missed you," he murmured against her skin.

"I should have been with you. I've been wishing I'd stayed ever since entering the railroad car in Brooklyn."

His lips claimed hers with a hunger that first surprised her, then drew a similar response.

She tipped back her head to smile into his face, and froze. Her heart constricted at the purple and garnet bruise on his cheekbone. She started to touch it, caught herself just in time, a moan working its way out of her throat. To think those awful kranks had hurt him!

She clutched his narrow, scratchy lapels and sought the truth to her question in his eyes. "Was it perfectly dreadful?"

One corner of his mustache moved up in a half-hearted smile. "Yes, it was, actually. The entire city of Brooklyn seemed to be against us. We took buggies to Washington Park Tuesday, dressed in uniform and ready to play, but the match was postponed on account of rain."

"I know. Frank told me."

He held her off, staring at her, astonishment written large across his face. "You asked Frank about the match?"

She played with a button on his coat, keeping her eyes carefully from his, embarrassed to admit the truth after her objections to Frank and the Irish Stars for so many years.

"I was worried about you and knew he'd have early news over the telegraph service."

He chuckled, and she looked up at him, sticking out her chin belligerently. "I may wish that he'd become a tee-totaler and give up the Irish Stars, and he may wish I would become a not-so-secret tippler, but we both love you. He understood that I wanted to know what was happening."

"Why you old fraud! After all these years, you've gone and become a true kranklet!"

"Don't be absurd." She shoved against his chest without effect. "It's not Base Ball which interests me, but a certain base baller by the name of Riley."

His eyes twinkling with laughter, he bent until his lips all but touched hers. "This Riley only *interests* you?" He kissed one edge of her mouth lightly, then the other.

"Well. . . " her arms slipped around his neck. She began to return his kisses, but he pulled his head back slightly.

"Well, what?" he teased.

"I love you, Dexter Riley."

"That's what I've needed to hear," he whispered, and kissed her tenderly, thoroughly.

Minutes later she reluctantly pulled away. "We're having guests for dinner; Frank and his wife, and Amanda, and Mr. Browning."

He looked at her in surprise, and she was grateful he didn't comment on her unusual guest list.

"I hope you aren't too tired for company after your trip. Your family and friends don't see you often enough, and they were eager to come by."

He shook his head slowly. "No, I'm not too tired."

The gentle, joy-filled look in his eyes was ample reward for the evening ahead.

Hours later, Dexter closed the large oak door with its etched bevel glass behind their guests, the pleasure of their company still warm inside him. It had been good to visit with his brother and sister-in-law in his home again.

He slipped his arm around Carrie and looked down at her black curls as she tucked her cheek against his shoulder. What had persuaded her to invite Frank and his wife after all these years? She'd been comfortable with them, too, not stiff and prim the way she used to be around his family. Whatever the reason for her change of heart, he was all for it.

"I'm glad you invited them," he said, starting toward the parlor with his arm still around her. He liked the secure, comfortable feeling it gave him to have her at his side like this.

She stepped away from his arm when they reached the parlor, and began to gather cups and saucers. He took the stack from her hands, setting them on the carved rosewood table in the middle of the room. "Leave them. I want to visit with my wife. Haven't seen her for a few days, you know, and she looks mighty pretty in that rose-colored dress."

He caught her hand, pulling her down beside him on the sofa, enjoying the color and sweet laughter his comment caused. He dropped a light kiss on the tip of her nose. "You were a wonderful hostess tonight, me love. I think you even charmed Browning. He was certainly on his best behaviour."

"I'm sure that's due to Amanda's charms, not mine."

He slid his arm around her shoulders and leaned his head against hers, her fragrant hair soft against his cheek. "Maybe. I never thought he'd still be escorting her after all these years."

"They don't see each other exclusively."

"No. Don't expect Browning will ever settle down to one woman." The fact Browning escorted Amanda at all made his stomach decidedly quesy. But she was a grown woman. There wasn't much he could do, except warn her. He'd tried that, but it had only made Amanda angry. He wished for the hundredth time that Grant had married her. "Did you hear about his fishing escapade?"

"No."

"Got so drunk, he went fishing in a rainstorm, in the gutter in front of his hotel." He snorted, frustration pouring through him. "I want someone better than that for Amanda."

She shifted in his arms, and cupped his cheek with one hand. "I know, my love. But perhaps she feels the good she sees in him outweighs the bad. Don't forget that Mr. Browning saved a boy's life a few years ago, when he pulled the child from beneath a moving streetcar." She dropped a quick kiss on his lips and stood. "Now, I must be getting those dirty dishes to the kitchen."

He watched as she went quickly about her business, the swish of her rose silk gentle beneath the clatter of china.

It wasn't like Carrie to champion his friends. He was accustomed to hearing her list their faults, not their virtues. He knew she still believed in people holding themselves to high standards. So what had changed her attitude?

seventeen

1891

"Now I lay me down to sleep. . ."

Dexter leaned against the door frame, hands in his pockets, and smiled at the homey scene. Carrie knelt between Benjy and Margaret beside the bed scattered with dolls and toys. The children were in their nightclothes, their hair still damp from their Saturday night baths.

Their backs were to him, but he could hear the children just fine, reciting their evening prayer in unison—though Benjy spoke with a slight lisp due to the tooth he'd lost earlier that day.

The scene struck a familiar chord. He remembered his own mother kneeling beside him, listening to his childhood prayers.

Was that why he'd fallen in love with Carrie, because she reminded him of her mother? She was lovely, sweet, and a sincere Christian, just like his mother had been.

A sense of loneliness settled across his chest like a fog; a loneliness he hadn't been consciously aware of in years. He missed his parents. He wished he'd had the chance to know them as an adult.

What would his mother think of the man her son had grown into, the man whose little-boy prayers she'd listened to every night before bed? A discomfort akin to shame wormed through him. Carrie had told him often that his mother would have been proud of the man he'd become, but he expected his mother would be mightily disappointed to know he'd not only abandoned the church, but the loving Christ about Whom she'd taught him.

Only the church people hadn't loved the saloon-keeper's

family. He tried to push away the thought. Wouldn't he ever get over that pain? He was a grown man with a family of his own. Time to put away childhood's hurts.

With a sigh, he crossed his arms over his chest, and concentrated on his own children while Margaret finished her "bless you's" and Benjy started on his, tripping a bit over his new lisp.

"God bless Mother and Father, Margaret, and Grandpa and Grandma Chambers, and Joey, and the Browns and the Rangers."

Dexter grinned. Trust Benjy to stick in both their ball clubs.

"And please make Daddy come to church and be a good man. Amen."

Dexter felt his face grow stiff as he watched Benjy jump to his feet and start to climb up on the bed.

'Benjy." Carrie stopped the boy with a gentle hand on his back. "Why did you pray that just now, about your father?"

"Our Sunday school teacher said people are supposed to go to church." He looked into her face with a sober, old man expression and batted his ridiculously long eyelashes once. "I don't want God to be mad at Daddy."

Dexter swallowed the lump that had suddenly appeared in his throat and shivered. His son thought he was a sinner. Well, he was, of course, but he wasn't quite ready for Benjy to give up his hero worship of him yet.

Margaret still knelt on the braided rug, elbows against the side of the quilt-covered mattress, resting her pointed little chin on her chubby hands, watching Benjy and Carrie intently. Carrie remained beside her, one hand rubbing Benjy's back. Dexter wished he could see her face. What was she thinking?

"Benjy, your father is a wonderful man."

"But our Sunday School teacher said it's a sin when people don't go to church."

"Yes, but we all have faults, Benjy. You must always remember that your father loves us, and takes very good care of us. He sees that we have lots of good food to eat, and nice clothes to wear, and a beautiful house to live in." She paused and brushed a damp lock of dark hair back from his forehead. "You have one of the best fathers on earth."

"But I can still pray for him to go to church, can't I?"

"Yes, Benjy."

Dexter heard her sigh just before he turned and headed down the stairs toward the parlor. Wave after wave of fury and despair swept over him. His jaw ached from his clenched teeth. He wasn't ready to lose his son's respect. He *wouldn't* lose it, even if it meant eating his words and attending church.

❧

Dexter chanced a sideways glance at Benjy, seated beside him in the pew, looking uncharacteristically angelic in his light blue suit, the huge white collar of his shirt lying about his shoulders like a mantle. The grin was still there; that huge grin that hadn't left the boy's face once since he'd seen his father arrive at the breakfast table dressed for church.

Likely the urchin thought his prayer was solely responsible for his father's presence. Well, it was, he admitted to himself, but not in the way the boy thought.

He stared at the picture above the altar. He couldn't help but feel like the entire congregation was watching him instead of listening to Rev. Chambers' sermon. Likely just his stupid pride. Why should anyone but Benjy, Carrie, and Rev. Chambers care whether he was here, or notice the many times he hadn't been over the last few years?

Was Carrie as uncomfortable around his Base Ball friends as he was at church? He always felt the church members were weighing him and finding him wanting, though they never actually said anything to make him feel that way. Did she feel the same about his friends, knowing they didn't share her values? She used to complain bitterly over his friendships. He'd only thought she was being uppity. It had never occurred to him before that he was asking anything difficult of her in expecting her to spend time with his friends.

Or had it? Had he wanted to see whether she could follow the Golden Rule with people who weren't like her?

He shrugged away the disconcerting thought and ran a finger beneath his starched collar, keeping his eyes carefully trained on the painting. Wasn't hearing a word of the sermon. He'd given himself a good talking-to last night and this morning; figured that was about as much of a sermon as he could take in one week.

It was hard to make regular conversation at the dinner table later. He and Carrie were both trying too hard to avoid mention of his church attendance, he realized. Smiling too brightly and laughing too long at small comments across the table set with the best china and crystal she always used for Sunday dinner.

When Benjy and Margaret were given permission to leave the table, they dashed toward the hall. Benjy stopped in the doorway and turned back, that huge smile still in place. "I'm glad you came to church today, Daddy."

A moment later he was racing out the front door after Margaret. The children's voices and laughter drifted through the open windows along with the spicy scents of early autumn.

Dexter took a deep breath and finally met Carrie's gaze. "And I was beginning to believe I was going to make it through the entire day without any of you commenting on it."

"I'm glad you came to church today, too." Her eyes were filled with joy, just as he'd known they would be, and guilt flooded through him, just as he'd known it would.

He crumpled his linen napkin into a ball with one hand and dropped it beside his plate. He tried to speak softly, even though his trampled pride was trying to send up angry signals. "I haven't had a change of heart. I went to church because I heard Benjy's prayer last night."

Was it pain that shot across her eyes? He felt the soft touch of her hand on his. "I'm sorry, Dexter. I wish you hadn't heard."

She was sorry? She'd defended him gallantly.

"A lad shouldn't have any cause to be ashamed of his Da. If

it will keep Benjy from being embarrassed of me, I'll even go to church gladly." He jerked his gaze from her, expecting that like his voice, his eyes showed anger, not gladness.

"Your son has no reason to be ashamed of you." Her fingers caressed the back of his hand as lightly as a feather, as soothing as her soft voice. "I'm sorry some church members were cruel to you when you were a boy."

Surprise locked his gaze on their hands. She knew him so well. He hadn't realized she understood how deeply he'd been hurt as a lad.

"Church isn't a place people go because they are better than others," she was continuing. "At least, it shouldn't be. I think it's a place people go because they realize they aren't good enough or strong enough to get through this life alone. It's a place for people to reach out to God and each other, not shun each other. Benjy has to learn that."

He stood, still reeling from the knowledge that she knew his deepest secret. Too deep and still too painful to discuss, even with Carrie.

Turning to the window near the table, he looked through the lace undercurtains into the yard where Margaret and Benjy were already playing with the neighbor children. It was time he apologized to Carrie. *Past* time. He'd never have the courage to if he had to look into her eyes when he did so, not after all these years.

"It shouldn't have taken Benjy's prayer to get me to church. I promised ye years ago that I'd always attend with ye." Wouldn't ye know that Irish would slip in again? Could never make a comment sound off-hand with that accent betraying him. "My behavior must have embarrassed ye with your own Da, him being a reverend."

The silence grew long. Wasn't she going to respond? He glanced over his shoulder. She was still seated at the table, staring at him. Tears shimmered in her eyes. How could such fragile things as teardrops have the power to stab through him?

He turned toward her, guilt filling him, and held out one hand.

She came to him without hesitation, and he pulled her back against his chest, where he could continue hiding from her eyes. Not that those beautiful, tear-filled eyes accused him. It was the lack of accusation there that cut through him, making him feel more of a cad than ever.

He leaned his cheek against her hair, the light, sweet fragrance of her lily-of-the-valley cologne filling his senses. "I've resented your church-going, Carrie. And resented the time ye've spent with your church friends. Don't be thinkin' I've not been noticing ye've given up time ye'd rather be spending with them to help with the boys' Base Ball club, and watch me play, and entertain my friends."

Her hands squeezed his where they lay at her waist. "It's no sacrifice to spend time with you, me love."

He kissed her temple. "I'm not so sure. I know how uncomfortable I feel around church goers. Ye're probably just as uncomfortable around my Base Ball friends."

"Perhaps I was at one time. But you're careful to insist they act like gentlemen around me and the children."

Dexter grimaced. He wasn't as noble as she believed. True, he'd told his friends that drinking, swearing, and off-color jokes weren't allowed in his home, but he'd let them believe he was simply honoring his wife's wishes. He hadn't stood up to the men and admitted that he didn't want such behavior around his wife and children.

"I broke my promise to ye. I'll not be breakin' it again."

"Dexter!"

He winced at the joy in her cry and hugged her closer, preventing her from turning to face him. "Mind ye, I'll not be attending every church event, but when Der Boss allows, I'll be in the pew beside ye on Sunday mornings."

"Thank you, my love."

A new peace filled him. It was such a little thing to make her so happy. Why had he resisted it so long?

❧

Working on a needlepoint wallhanging of the love chapter four months later with Hope's cheerful canary song a background for her thoughts, she still couldn't believe it. Dexter had accompanied them to services every Sunday since that day in November. She hadn't dared comment on his attendance for fear he would become embarrassed and quit coming.

He didn't attend any of the other church activities, but at least he was once again hearing God's Word on a regular basis. Did he allow himself to open his heart and mind to it, or did he continue to rebel against God inside while faithfully joining them in the pews each Sunday?

Footsteps hurried across the wide wooden floor of the porch which swept around the front and sides of the house. The front door flew open. A cold March wind breezed into the parlor to greet her along with Dexter's eager voice.

"Carrie, look who I've brought home!"

She'd barely left the tapestry-covered, armless oak rocker before he arrived in the room with another man in tow, both in popular, finely checked brown sack suits. Dexter tossed his derby to a small inlaid table, while the guest removed his, revealing neat, short-cropped brown hair above a wide forehead. The man, who couldn't be more than thirty, did look vaguely familiar.

Dexter's mustache rode his wide grin. "Remember the man who beat our fresh third baseman out of a pile of money in a foot race a few years back?"

"Of course! Billy Sunday! Welcome to our home. Have you joined the Browns?"

"Browns aren't so fortunate as that, lass. He's here to speak at the Young Men's Christian Association."

"That's right, Mrs. Riley. We're organizing Base Ball clubs for boys at Y's across the country. Many of the larger cities already have clubs. In spite of the way professional Base Ball has become a cesspool of greed, the sport itself is clean, and lends itself to producing a healthy body. I believe if boys have Base Ball to occupy themselves, they won't become involved in occupations more conducive to temptations."

She glanced at Dexter. "Dexter has advised a group of boys in the neighborhood with their Base Ball club for years. I must admit, they use every spare moment for the sport and not one boy has yet developed into a troublesome youngster. However, I do fear for when they are older, attend matches regularly, and are exposed to beer sold on every side."

His straight mouth widened in a smile, and his eyes flashed with friendliness toward a recognized sympathizer. "I agree. One of the next fights must be against liquor at the ball grounds. And along with that, the outlawing of Sunday ball."

"You'll have a tough time with those fights. Men like Der Boss consider beer and Sunday ball the edges that add the profit to their pockets." Dexter waved a broad hand toward his favorite overstuffed chair. "Sit down, man. Make yourself comfortable."

Billy took the chair offered, and Dexter dropped onto the green velvet sofa opposite. Carrie lowered herself to the rocker once again.

"What do you think about beer and Sunday ball?" Billy's direct gaze beneath straight dark brows challenged Dexter, though his tone was conversational.

"I wouldn't mind spending Sunday afternoons with my wife and family." He smiled at her, and their gazes tangled. Somehow he'd made the simple statement an intimate, sentimental admission that wrapped her in love. He glanced back at Sunday. "And as to beer, I'm a bit tired of kranks throwing steins at the players when they don't like what's happening on the grounds."

Billy's laugh filled the room. It was a pleasant laugh, Carrie thought, full and rich.

"In case you hadn't noticed," Dexter informed her, "Billy has gotten a little religion."

Billy shrugged good-naturedly. "More like a lot of religion."

"And, it doesn't disturb you?" she asked hesitantly. "Your involvement in a profession which promotes beer and Sunday ball?"

"I play in the National League. They don't allow beer served in their ball grounds, you may remember. As for Sunday ball, after committing my life to the Lord, I insist my contracts stipulate I won't be required to play on Sundays."

Dexter, who had been listening with his chin resting on one hand, leaned forward. "Your owner actually signed such a contract?"

Billy smiled. "I have a more powerful Owner than the owner of the Cubs."

"I'm serious."

"So am I. But yes, the Cubs owner signed it, and he sticks by it."

Dexter rubbed one of his thick knuckles back and forth beneath his chin, his eyes thoughtful. "Of course, no owner would want to lose a talented player like yourself." He shoved a thumb in Billy's direction and glanced at Carrie. "He stole eighty-four bases this year."

"I'm planning to leave Base Ball. I've been asked to work with the Young Mens' Christian Association full-time. I've enjoyed the sport, but helping to shape boys' lives is more important to me. Because of my Base Ball fame, the kids listen to what I say."

"The boys in our neighborhood are the same with Dexter. They actually seek him out for advice." Carrie couldn't keep the pride from her voice.

Sunday snapped his fingers. "Say, why don't you join forces with me at the program this evening, Dex? Sounds like the Lord already has you working with St. Louis' boys."

"I'm not much of one for talking about God. Wouldn't know what to say."

"Well, come along with me, anyway."

"Sure, if you'll stay with us tonight, instead of at a hotel. Give us a chance to visit some more before your train leaves tomorrow. How about if Carrie and the kids come along with us tonight?"

"The more the merrier."

"There's someone I'd like you to meet before we leave for the meeting. A neighbor boy, Joey. Loves Base Ball. Doctor says he'll never play it again, though."

Billy agreed immediately, and the two set off together with a copy of the new dime novel *Muldoon's Base Ball Club in Philadelphia*, which Dexter had picked up for the boy. It was a humorous book, but she knew Dexter found particularly amusing the fact that Muldoon's Base Ball club was Irish.

Carrie couldn't quell the hope that rose inside her, sending an excited buzz along her nerves while she prepared herself and the children for the evening. Listening to Billy tell the audience how his faith in God had changed his life, would her husband finally open his mind and heart to God, also? She could barely pray that he would, for the hope was so strong. After eight years of praying and hoping and waiting and loving, was tonight the night Dexter would accept God's gifts of love and salvation?

The room hummed with excitement that evening. Boys from five through twenty-five came to hear Billy speak. They howled with appreciation when he entered the stage, sliding across the polished oak floor in a stimulating rendition of his famous base-stealing play. They laughed when he told of praying he would make a pennant-winning catch while running over benches and through spectators.

There wasn't a single deriding hoot from the audience when he told how his faith in Christ had changed his life, and how He could change their lives. When he asked anyone who wanted to make a decision to live for God to come forward, Carrie held her breath until she thought her chest would burst, hoping Dexter would join those walking up the aisles.

He didn't.

When they sat up until the early morning hours talking, they didn't discuss the Lord, either. At least not while she was with them. Instead they talked Base Ball: the new Players League formed in opposition to the $2,500 salary cap set by both

National League and American Association owners, the many players deserting the National League for the Players League, rumors of gambling on Base Ball matches, Von der Ahe's suspicions of match throwing and subsequent player fines, mass desertion by most of the Browns for the new Players League and the Browns' surprisingly good third-place showing in spite of it. And their shared disappointment at the way things were deteriorating within the game they both loved.

Knowing Billy, she was sure he would confront Dexter about her husband's faith when she left them and went to bed. She arose in the morning hoping to hear Dexter had discovered the joy of Christ's salvation. But neither man mentioned that Dexter had had a change of heart.

"I had such high hopes over Billy's visit," she whispered, watching between parlor draperies as the two men left together for Union Depot.

The canary's song gaily spilled through the parlor. Carrie walked to the tall brass cage. The bird's yellow feathers were a cheerful note in the otherwise darkly decorated room. Hope tipped its head, eyeing her curiously, then continued its song.

"Are you reprimanding me for being such a poor sport? The St. Louis Browns would never have won so many pennants if they gave up as easily as me, would they? 'Love never faileth.' Hope 'never stops—at all.' Thank you kindly for the reminder."

eighteen

1892

Carrie slipped her arms into the loose-fitting top of soft, dove gray merino that buttoned discreetly up the front beneath boxy pleats which hung over the top of her skirt. She loved the freedom pregnancy gave her from her binding corsets, which seemed to grow tighter each year.

She rested her hands lightly on her stomach. *A baby.* There had been a time when she'd doubted she and Dexter would ever have another child.

That was almost five years ago, when Emmet had said, "Don't give up on him."

She hadn't given up. She hadn't won yet, either.

Of course she hadn't, she corrected herself. There is no winning or losing in love. There is only loving.

She patted the top where it hung loosely over her bulging middle. "I hope you marry someone as nice as your daddy, but someone who loves Jesus."

She laughed at herself. She'd teased Grant and Dexter about worrying over their daughters' future husbands while the girls were newborns, and here she was doing the same thing, only this child wasn't even born.

The bedroom door opened, and she turned toward it in surprise. Her heart lurched. Dexter stood staring at her, one hand gripping the brass knob. His usually sun-warmed skin was gray. His eyes burned with shock and confusion.

Fear shot through her. She wanted to shut the moment out of time. She didn't want to know the terrible thing he knew.

"What is it?"

"Joey. The nurse who's been staying with the lad just stopped.

The doctor said. . .he's in a bad way. His only chance is surgery, and that's for bein' dangerous at best."

Joey! It didn't seem possible.

"His parents sent a message. Joey wants us to come."

They brought the children along. In case the worst happened, Benjy must have the opportunity to see his friend one last time.

He's stronger about this than we are, she thought later, watching the boys together.

Joey's skin was almost as pale as the pillows against which he was propped in his narrow bed. He was so slender that his body barely made a dent in the bedding. His breathing was shallow and shaky, and she wondered whether they should tax his strength when he needed every ounce of it so badly.

Benjy sat on the stool that allowed him to visit on an equal height with Joey. She knew his frequent visits had taught him that it was painful for Joey to be jostled about, so he didn't attempt to sit on the bed.

"You can have that book we finished reading yesterday if you want to, Ben."

"The one about Double Curve Dan, the Base Ball detective?"

"Yeah."

"That was a good story. The other guys on the club will prob'ly like it, too."

Carrie heard Dexter, standing beside her with Margaret in his arms, swallow hard. "Going to tell Joey the news about the club, Benjy?"

"Oh, yeah!" He leaned forward eagerly, his green eyes sparkling beneath his long lashes, a healthy flush on his cheeks that made her feel guilty to have a son who was so alive. "The nine voted yesterday. We're not going to be the Rangers any more. We're going to be Joey's Rangers."

The tiniest hint of color touched Joey's drawn cheeks. "Honest?"

Benjy gave a sharp nod. "Honest. You're the one who got us started, remember?"

The pale lips quivered in a smile. "I like Base Ball. Say, you be sure ta practice that throw Tony Mullane taught you. Maybe one day you'll be a champion hurler like he is."

"Think I might?"

"Sure. If ya practice every day like I always tell ya."

"Benjy," Dexter's voice was low, but Benjy heard and understood.

He slid down from the oak stool and stood as close to the bed as possible without leaning against it. "Guess I better go." He took one of Joey's hands carefully in his own and gave it a gentle, solemn shake. "'Bye."

"'Bye."

Dexter touched Benjy's shoulder. "Will you and Margaret wait in the hall, Benjy? Your mother and I will be out soon."

When the door closed behind the children, she and Dexter moved from the foot of the bed to the side.

"He likes ta be called Ben now."

She smiled at Joey's gentle reprimand. So like him to be watching out for Benjy—Ben—even now.

"We'll try to remember." Dexter's voice sounded thick.

Joey nodded slightly. Closed his eyes.

The simple motion sent fear darting through her. The few words he'd spoken with Benjy had cost him dearly in strength.

His eyes opened again, and distress washed over her when she noticed that his skin was almost as blue as his eyes. "He's a good kid."

Still speaking of Benjy. Ben.

Dexter nodded. One of his large hands massaged his neck. She wondered whether his throat was as tight as hers, whether he was having difficulty getting words through it. "Yeah." The word wasn't much more than a hoarse whisper.

He cleared his throat, and laid a hand gently on Joey's shoulder. "Ye're one of the reasons he's a good kid, and a good base baller, too. Ye look out for him just like a big brother would. Means a lot to me, knowing ye're watching out for him, 'specially since I have to be away at match games so often."

The edge of a smile touched the thin lips. Pride shone in the tired eyes.

Her own eyes burned from trying to hold back tears. Were they as red as Dexter's? His had an unusual sheen to them.

He dug one hand deep into his trousers pocket and took Joey's hand with the other. The boy's fingers looked tiny, white, and helpless beside his.

A tear rolled over Dexter's lashes and down his dark cheek. At the sight of it, her own tears escaped. Not once in all the years they'd been together had she seen him cry!

"Don't worry, Cap. Doc's pretty good, and if he can't fix me, I'm not afraid ta die. I trust in Jesus, just like ya said I should. I know He'll take care of me."

She swallowed hard, trying not to sob. Joey was being so brave. She didn't want to make it harder for him.

Suddenly his words penetrated her mind, and she gasped. Dexter had told him to trust in Jesus?

"Ya think there's Base Ball in heaven, Cap?"

A shaky laugh burst from Dexter. "I'm not for knowing much about what heaven's like. All I know is that 'tis a good place, where people aren't for hurting each other, and we never have to say good-bye. But I expect since Jesus was a little boy on earth once Himself, He'll not be objectin' too strenuously to a Base Ball match now and then."

"Clouds will be pretty soft for sliding into base on, don't ya think?"

Joey's words came back to her that evening after they'd tucked the children in bed. She hoped it would be a long time before Joey discovered whether the clouds were soft to slide upon.

She followed Dexter into the parlor, where a fat, rose-shaded lamp shed deceptively mellow light through the properly stiff room. He stopped in the middle of the colorful Persian carpet, his hands clenching and unclenching, again and again, at his sides.

She slid her arms around his waist, wishing she could draw his pain away, into herself.

He reacted instantly to her touch, burying his face in her neck, crushing her shoulders in his embrace. Warm tears dampened her skin and the collar of the gray merino top she'd donned with such joy that morning.

The desperation in his manner spoke louder than the words she knew he would say if he could: "I love him." "I've never felt so helpless." "What if it were Benjy?"

She drew him down on the couch. They held each other all the night through.

Not once did she consider moving, even when her arms fell asleep from cradling him.

Not once did she ask about the faith in Jesus to which he and Joey had alluded, though her spirit cried out to know when he had accepted the freeing belief for which she had prayed so many years.

Not once did she get up to cover Hope's cage, the canary Joey had brought to their home, a symbol of their love and commitment; the canary who sang them gentle songs of comfort throughout the night, and never stopped—at all.

❧

Joey didn't discover that year whether clouds were soft to slide upon, but his recovery was slow.

In the days after learning he would live, Dexter seemed filled with unbounded joy. Carrie waited eagerly for him to mention the faith she'd learned of at Joey's bedside.

He didn't.

The longer she waited, the more difficult it was to broach the subject. She was on the well-known pins and needles, watching for signs he was becoming more like Grant and her father and Emmet.

She hesitated before saying grace at meals, hoping he would eagerly step in to express their thanks.

He didn't.

She read her Bible while sitting beside him in the parlor evenings, hoping he would offer to read with her.

He didn't.

After two months, she could stand it no longer, and asked him straight out when he had changed his mind and heart about the Lord.

One edge of his mouth beneath the closely trimmed, wine-red mustache lifted in the self-conscious smile so different from his usual grin. He turned his sparkling gaze away for a moment, then returned it to her in the familiar manner that spoke of his unease.

"One day I found myself talking to Him." He snorted and shook his head. "Talking to Someone I didn't believe existed. Suppose that was the start of it."

He pulled her closer, until her head rested against his chest. She knew he was hiding from her his eyes and face with their revealing natures.

"I asked Him that night to show me if He was real. It was a long time before I realized He was showing me Himself through your love, girleen. I thought I wanted something bold to happen, like when God appeared to the apostle Paul." He pulled back slightly, allowing her to look into his face for a moment, and grinned. "Ye see, I have been listening to your Da's sermons."

His fingers slid through her hair, cupping the back of her head, and urged her cheek back against the cool linen of his shirt.

"God had a better way in mind for me. He showed me what it's like to be truly loved."

She blinked at the tears that suddenly filled her lashes, and hugged him tighter while he cleared the huskiness from his throat.

"When ye first told me ye loved me, I was. . .overwhelmed. In spite of the saloon, even though I was a base ballist, ye loved me. And then ye told me ye wouldn't be marrying me because

I didn't share your faith, and all the old hurts I'd known as a lad came rushing back."

She caught back a cry, distress pouring through her.

"Shhh, lass." His breath was warm against her hair. "It's all right now."

"But I never meant to hurt you so!"

"I know, love. Ye were only being true to your beliefs. And then ye agreed to marry me anyway." His fingers played with the hair at the back of her head, and he rested his cheek against her hair. "I knew it went against your beliefs to marry me, and because of that, I always felt ye were ashamed of me, that I wasn't quite good enough for ye."

"It was never that you weren't good enough!"

"I know that now. But I. . .I'm ashamed to be sayin' I was testing your love. I wanted ye to love me in spite of my faults. I think that's one of the reasons I stopped going to church, and why I fought God for so long. I knew your faith was the most important thing in your life. If you could love me even if I didn't share your faith, then I'd know your love was real. But I didn't truly believe it was that strong."

She strangled the protestation that rose to her throat.

"By our fifth anniversary, I figured I was right, that ye didn't love me, that ye wished ye'd married Emmet." His arms squeezed her tighter. "I'm sorry, me love. I wasn't fair to ye, or to God. Ye went against your father and your beliefs to marry me. Ye've stuck beside me even when I went against my word to you. Ye've befriended my friends when I shunned yours. Ye loved me and believed in me, even when I rejected your faith for all these years."

"But it's different now."

"Yes. One day I realized He'd shown me through ye how faithful His love is. Mother always told me not to judge church goers by the worst of the lot, but by the best. I never listened to that advice. Until you. So I asked God to forgive me, the way your Da is always saying people have to do, and thanked Him for sending Christ to bring me to Him."

"I'm so glad. But why haven't you told me before?"

Hands at her shoulders pushed her firmly away until he could meet her curious gaze. "I'm not good at talking about such things. Some things are too personal and. . .too difficult to explain." His eyes warmed, and he drew her back into his embrace. "Like my love for you," he whispered against her lips before claiming them.

Surrendering to his arms, she remembered the stars.

❧

Lafayette Park was as beautiful in fall as in May, Carrie thought, looking about at the lovely blend of muted bronzes, golds, and crimsons surrounding them in the trees and among the fallen leaves. The colors reflected in the pond, where leaves drifted lazily along on the top of water barely rippled by the slight breeze which carried the spicy, moldering scent of autumn on its wings.

It had been May, with the air thick with the scent of lilacs, and everything newly green, the first time she'd been here with Dexter. It would always be lovely to her. The first time he'd told her he loved her had been in this place.

That was ten years ago. It hardly seemed possible. So many things had changed, not the least of which was the existence of their children, who were merely hazy dreams when the two of them fell in love. Now nine-year-old Ben and almost eight-year-old Margaret played along the water's edge with Dexter, while Joey sat watching them, still weak six months after his surgery. Three-month-old Joseph slept beside her peacefully wrapped in a pale green blanket of softest merino wool.

She brushed a crisp brown leaf from her skirt and smiled. Fashions had changed too, for which she gave bountiful thanks. The tightly bodiced gown with bindingly-close sleeves and the uncomfortable bustle which she'd worn the day she met Dexter had been replaced by a far more feminine suit. She removed her gloves, and smoothed her hands over the lavender and deep green figures on the cream background of her challis skirt. How nice that Dexter had insisted she treat herself to a new outfit now that Joseph had arrived and her figure was returning to something resembling her original size!

Dexter had changed, too. His mustache wasn't as large, and he was even suggesting the possibility of removing it completely. She hoped he wouldn't. She liked its softness against her skin when he kissed her. His hair wasn't as thick as it was ten years ago, or the color as wine-shaded. The lines at the outer edges of his eyes were deeply etched from years of playing Base Ball in the sun.

He had all but retired his black derby for the popular dark gray Boston with its creased crown and a black band above the wide brim. She had to admit, he looked handsome in it. The sight of him still set her heart tripping like a trotting carriage pony, the same as when they'd met.

The largest change was inside Dexter. She knew it was there. Knew it in the relaxed manner he had when they were in church. Knew it in the joyous comments he would occasionally make concerning the discovery of faith in another. But he still wasn't like most of the Christian men with whom she'd grown up.

He dropped down on the quilt beside her, surprising her from her thoughts and her gazing upon Joseph. He grinned, noting the direction her gaze had taken. "Still can't get enough of looking at him, even after three months of changing and feeding and staying up nights, can you?"

"No." She laughed.

"Neither can I."

She loved his sweet admission, loved the way his voice was thick with love for their child.

He ran a knuckle lightly along her cheek, his eyes shining into hers. "I like watching you watch him. Like being a mother, don't you?"

"Love it." She looked down at Joseph. She didn't dare look at Dexter when she made her request, for fear he'd be offended by her disappointment if he denied it. "I've been thinking of the service Grant and Phoebe had for Rose Marie. Would you mind if we had one for Joseph?"

"No, sounds like a fine idea. We should have had them for Ben and Margaret, too."

His quick agreement was a pleasant surprise.

"It would bring me comfort to know that together we've entrusted our children to the Lord."

He was watching Joseph, running the twig of a red maple leaf lightly over the blanket, and she knew he was somewhat embarrassed by the topic.

"Would. . .would you pray with me, Dexter?"

He glanced at her then, giving her a tight smile. "Sure."

He slipped an arm about her shoulders, and she leaned against him, resting her cheek on his afternoon frock coat. After a minute, he squeezed her shoulder and dropped his arm. "I love you," he said quietly with a self-conscious smile.

She gave him back a smile with trembling lips. It was always the same. She'd asked him to pray with her a handful of times since discovering his faith, and always it was just like this. He held her close, prayed silently, and afterward looked like he'd been caught pilfering the neighbors' apples.

At first it had disturbed her. Now, she was grateful he prayed with her, even if it wasn't in the manner to which she'd grown accustomed in her parents' home and in her friendship with Emmet. She would have preferred they pray aloud together, but the Lord had said that wherever two or more were gathered together in His name, He was there; that was all that was truly important.

"I think it's time I left Base Ball, Carrie."

She stared at him, stunned.

He slid a sideways glance at her and wiggled his eyebrows in his dear, funny way. "Think you can bear having your husband in town every night of the year?"

In spite of his smile, his eyes revealed her answer was

important to him. "I should love having my husband home every night. But why. . . "

"I told Der Boss I wanted a clause in my contract saying I needn't play Sunday ball. He said I wasn't important enough to the club to agree to such a concession."

"I'm sorry." Her heart thundered above her quiet words. To think he'd actually asked to be released from playing on the Sabbath! Surely the Lord was working in his life. But she hated that Mr. Von der Ahe would hurt him this way. "He was wrong about your importance, of course."

He smiled, his eyes warm with gratitude for her support, but shook his head. "I'm getting to be an old man in this sport. I've been playing Base Ball for sixteen years now. Those first years with the Browns, they were the best. But most of my friends have been sold to other clubs. Now that the American Association has merged with the National League, nothing is the same. Grant's offered me a position with his law firm, now that I have my degree. Like to move back to your home town, Carrie?"

"Sounds wonderful!" It was the only place she would want to live other than St. Louis. How good of the Lord to arrange it for the next step of their life together!

Dexter drew up his knees, leaned his elbows on them, and gave his attention to the children, who were busy pulling two small wooden tug boats about by strings through the shallows at the edge of the pond. "Remember your father's sermon this morning? Where Solomon asked God for wisdom, and God made him the wisest man to ever live?"

"Yes." *How unusual for him to discuss a sermon!*

"What would you ask for from God, if you could have only one thing?"

Your salvation. The words leaped to her mind. She had been praying for him to come to the Lord for so many years! But now the prayer had been answered.

There was another she'd almost forgotten. Ten years ago, before she'd known Dexter was returning to ask her to reconsider his marriage proposal, she'd made a request of God. She recalled the moment vividly: Standing in the parlor at the St. Louis parsonage, looking out on the cheerful fall garden, she'd begged, "Lord, if it is the only thing I learn in life, teach me to love as Thou dost love."

In the years since she'd begun studying the love chapter and seeking to be taught how to love, she'd not once remembered that prayer.

Her heart stood still. Beat on, as quickly as a hummingbird flutters its wings. Had God used her marriage to Dexter to answer her request? Would she have gone to the effort to love Dexter that she had these last years if she hadn't promised God to stay with Dexter for life?

He was still awaiting her answer, watching her with curiosity behind an unusual veil of reserve. She looked directly into his beautiful peridot-green eyes and put all the warmth she could into her gaze. "I'd ask Him to teach me to love you as much as He does, Dexter."

The veil of reserve dissolved. His eyes glistened suspiciously in the moment before he caught her to himself. "And I'd ask Him to make me worthy of your love, girleen." The admission was a husky whisper against her hair, a whisper that filled her chest with an aching desire to be able to express the tender love she felt.

She pulled back slightly, resting her head on his shoulder, looking up into his face, adoring him. Her hand touched his cheek. "You are worthy, just as you are."

The look that leaped to his eyes humbled her with its joy.

Contentment such as she'd never before experienced filled her. Perhaps Dexter would never be like other Christian men she knew. A small sigh escaped her at the thought of the sharing of the Word and in prayer that she might never know with him. But he was a child of God, and took wonderful care of her and the children, and in his own quiet, unobtrusive way, he touched people for Christ who weren't being touched by people like her.

Perhaps their marriage hadn't been God's perfect will. Perhaps she had made the wrong choice when she married him instead of Emmet. But God had helped her to honor the vows she'd taken, had helped her to learn to love the man she'd married.

Why had it taken so *long* to learn to love him?

She'd thought she loved him when they married, that the passion, the overwhelming desire for his presence and his arms, was love. She hadn't known anything about love then. It had taken ten years of struggling, choosing to act in a loving manner, to begin to know what love was all about. Doubtless the Lord had a great deal left to teach her on the subject.

A warm rush of tenderness flowed through her. The rewards of learning to love were well worth the lessons.

"It will be our tenth anniversary next Sunday, Dexter. I'm so lucky to be married to you."

A chuckle broke out above her ear. "I don't think you're lucky."

She pushed away from him, miffed.

He reached to pull her back but stopped when a middle-aged woman appeared on the walkway with a skinny little white dog on a lead. Dropping his arm casually about his knee, he leaned over to whisper, "I don't think we were lucky. I think it was planned."

Planned? Perhaps. Perhaps not. But it wasn't long ago he hadn't even believed in God, and now he believed God planned their love. Wasn't that a miracle?

Sweet joy snuggled down inside her, and curled up around her heart.

A Letter To Our Readers

Dear Reader:

In order that we might better contribute to your reading enjoyment, we would appreciate your taking a few minutes to respond to the following questions. When completed, please return to the following:

Rebecca Germany, Managing Editor
Heartsong Presents
P.O. Box 719
Uhrichsville, Ohio 44683

1. Did you enjoy reading *The Hope That Sings*?
   - ❑ Very much. I would like to see more books by this author!
   - ❑ Moderately
     I would have enjoyed it more if ________________

   ____

2. Are you a member of **Heartsong Presents**? ❑Yes ❑No
   If no, where did you purchase this book? ________________

   ____

3. What influenced your decision to purchase this book? (Check those that apply.)

❑ Cover	❑ Back cover copy
❑ Title	❑ Friends
❑ Publicity	❑ Other________________

4. How would you rate, on a scale from 1 (poor) to 5 (superior), the cover design? ________________

5. On a scale from 1 (poor) to 10 (superior), please rate the following elements.

___Heroine ___Plot

___Hero ___Inspirational theme

___Setting ___Secondary characters

6. What settings would you like to see covered in **Heartsong Presents** books?___________________

____

____

7. What are some inspirational themes you would like to see treated in future books?_______________

____

____

8. Would you be interested in reading other **Heartsong Presents** titles? ❑ Yes ❑ No

9. Please check your age range:
❑ Under 18 ❑ 18-24 ❑ 25-34
❑ 35-45 ❑ 46-55 ❑ Over 55

10. How many hours per week do you read? __________

Name ____

Occupation _____________________________________

Address ____

City_________________State__________Zip__________

JoAnn A. Grote

___ ***The Unfolding Heart***—As Millicent and Adam's attraction for each other grows, Millicent realizes she could never make a good wife for a minister. And even if she could, how could she ever bring herself to live with him amid the crudeness and danger of the frontier? HP51

___ ***Treasure of the Heart***—John Wells leaves his fiancée in Minnesota to go in search of the reason for his father's murder. Among the Black Hills of South Dakota he finds the answers he needs, as well as a rare treasure of the heart, Jewell Emerson. HP55

___ ***Love's Shining Hope***—As Pearl and Jason are drawn closer together in the worst of times, Pearl is faced with a decision like no other. Should she accept Jason's hasty proposal, well aware that he wants a marriage in name only to run the farm? HP103

___ ***An Honest Love***—Constance Ward's work as a Pinkerton agent requires secrecy and deception. Little does she realize that she will also be required to marry a total stranger. Joined before God under circumstances of fear and falsehood, Constance and Justin Knight struggle to accept each other without the benefit of loving trust. HP120

___ ***The Rekindled Flame***—Marian is happy to come to Minneapolis, where no one knows her scandalous history. Losing herself in exciting work with needy children at a local mission, Marian finds herself drawn to a fellow worker. and his daughter. HP136

Send to: Heartsong Presents Reader's Service
P.O. Box 719
Uhrichsville, Ohio 44683

Please send me the items checked above. I am enclosing **$2.95 for each title** totaling $_____(please add $1.00 to cover postage and handling per order. OH add 6.25% tax. NJ add 6% tax.).
Send check or money order, no cash or C.O.D.s, please.
To place a credit card order, call 1-800-847-8270.

NAME ______________________________

ADDRESS ______________________________

CITY/STATE ____________________ ZIP __________

Heartsong

Any 12 *Heartsong Presents* titles for only $26.95 **

**plus $1.00 shipping and handling per order and sales tax where applicable.

HISTORICAL ROMANCE IS CHEAPER BY THE DOZEN!

Buy any assortment of twelve *Heartsong Presents* titles and save 25% off of the already discounted price of $2.95 each!

HEARTSONG PRESENTS TITLES AVAILABLE NOW:

_HP 39 RAINBOW HARVEST, *Norene Morris*
_HP 40 PERFECT LOVE, *Janelle Jamison*
_HP 43 VEILED JOY, *Colleen L. Reece*
_HP 44 DAKOTA DREAM, *Lauraine Snelling*
_HP 51 THE UNFOLDING HEART, *JoAnn A. Grote*
_HP 55 TREASURE OF THE HEART, *JoAnn A. Grote*
_HP 56 A LIGHT IN THE WINDOW, *Janelle Jamison*
_HP 59 EYES OF THE HEART, *Maryn Langer*
_HP 60 MORE THAN CONQUERORS, *Kay Cornelius*
_HP 63 THE WILLING HEART, *Janelle Jamison*
_HP 64 CROWS'-NESTS AND MIRRORS, *Colleen L. Reece*
_HP 67 DAKOTA DUSK, *Lauraine Snelling*
_HP 68 RIVERS RUSHING TO THE SEA, *Jacquelyn Cook*
_HP 71 DESTINY'S ROAD, *Janelle Jamison*
_HP 72 SONG OF CAPTIVITY, *Linda Herring*
_HP 75 MUSIC IN THE MOUNTAINS, *Colleen L. Reece*
_HP 76 HEARTBREAK TRAIL, *VeraLee Wiggins*
_HP 87 SIGN OF THE BOW, *Kay Cornelius*
_HP 88 BEYOND TODAY, *Janelle Jamison*
_HP 91 SIGN OF THE EAGLE, *Kay Cornelius*
_HP 92 ABRAM MY LOVE, *VeraLee Wiggins*
_HP 95 SIGN OF THE DOVE, *Kay Cornelius*
_HP 96 FLOWER OF SEATTLE, *Colleen L. Reece*
_HP 99 ANOTHER TIME...ANOTHER PLACE, *Bonnie L. Crank*
_HP100 RIVER OF PEACE, *Janelle Burnham*
_HP103 LOVE'S SHINING HOPE, *JoAnn A. Grote*
_HP104 HAVEN OF PEACE, *Carol Mason Parker*
_HP107 PIONEER LEGACY, *Norene Morris*
_HP108 LOFTY AMBITIONS, *Diane L. Christner*
_HP111 A KINGDOM DIVIDED, *Tracie J. Peterson*
_HP112 CAPTIVES OF THE CANYON, *Colleen L. Reece*
_HP115 SISTERS IN THE SUN, *Shirley Rhode*
_HP116 THE HEART'S CALLING, *Tracie J. Peterson*
_HP119 BECKONING STREAMS, *Janelle Burnham*
_HP120 AN HONEST LOVE, *JoAnn A. Grote*
_HP123 THE HEART HAS ITS REASONS, *Birdie L. Etchison*
_HP124 HIS NAME ON HER HEART, *Mary LaPietra*

(If ordering from this page, please remember to include it with the order form.)

Presents

__HP127 FOREVER YOURS, *Tracie J. Peterson*
__HP128 MISPLACED ANGEL, *VeraLee Wiggins*
__HP131 LOVE IN THE PRAIRIE WILDS, *Robin Chandler*
__HP132 LOST CREEK MISSION, *Cheryl Tenbrook*
__HP135 SIGN OF THE SPIRIT, *Kay Cornelius*
__HP136 REKINDLED FLAME, *JoAnn A. Grote*
__HP140 ANGEL'S CAUSE, *Tracie J. Peterson*
__HP143 MORNING MOUNTAIN, *Peggy Darty*
__HP144 FLOWER OF THE WEST, *Colleen L. Reece*
__HP147 DREWRY'S BLUFF, *Cara McCormack*
__HP148 DREAMS OF THE PIONEERS, *Linda Herring*
__HP151 FOLLOW THE LEADER, *Loree Lough*
__HP152 BELATED FOLLOWER, *Colleen L. Reece*
__HP155 TULSA TEMPEST, *Norma Jean Lutz*
__HP156 FLY AWAY HOME, *Jane LaMunyon*
__HP159 FLOWER OF THE NORTH, *Colleen L. Reece*
__HP160 TO KEEP FAITH, *Carolyn R. Scheidies*
__HP163 DREAMS OF GLORY, *Linda Herring*
__HP164 ALAS MY LOVE, *Tracie J. Peterson*
__HP167 PRISCILLA HIRES A HUSBAND, *Loree Lough*
__HP168 LOVE SHALL COME AGAIN, *Birdie L. Etchison*
__HP171 TULSA TURNING, *Norma Jean Lutz*
__HP172 A WHISPER OF SAGE, *Esther Loewen Vogt*
__HP175 JAMES'S JOY, *Cara McCormack*
__HP176 WHERE THERE IS HOPE, *Carolyn R. Scheidies*
__HP179 HER FATHER'S LOVE, *Nancy Lavo*
__HP180 FRIEND OF A FRIEND, *Jill Richardson*
__HP183 A NEW LOVE, *VeraLee Wiggins*
__HP184 THE HOPE THAT SINGS, *JoAnn A. Grote*

Great Inspirational Romance at a Great Price!

Heartsong Presents books are inspirational romances in contemporary and historical settings, designed to give you an enjoyable, spirit-lifting reading experience. You can choose wonderfully written titles from some of today's best authors like Peggy Darty, Colleen L. Reece, Tracie J. Peterson, VeraLee Wiggins, and many others.

When ordering quantities less than twelve, above titles are $2.95 each.

SEND TO: Heartsong Presents Reader's Service
P.O. Box 719, Uhrichsville, Ohio 44683

Please send me the items checked above. I am enclosing $________.
(please add $1.00 to cover postage per order. OH add 6.25% tax. NJ add 6%). Send check or money order, no cash or C.O.D.s, please.

To place a credit card order, call 1-800-847-8270.

NAME ______________________________

ADDRESS ______________________________

CITY/STATE ______________________ **ZIP** ________

HPS 8-96

Hearts♥ng Presents

Love Stories Are Rated G!

That's for godly, gratifying, and of course, great! If you love a thrilling love story, but don't appreciate the sordidness of some popular paperback romances, **Heartsong Presents** is for you. In fact, **Heartsong Presents** is the *only inspirational romance book club*, the only one featuring love stories where Christian faith is the primary ingredient in a marriage relationship.

Sign up today to receive your first set of four, never before published Christian romances. Send no money now; you will receive a bill with the first shipment. You may cancel at any time without obligation, and if you aren't completely satisfied with any selection, you may return the books for an immediate refund!

Imagine. . .four new romances every four weeks—two historical, two contemporary—with men and women like you who long to meet the one God has chosen as the love of their lives. . .all for the low price of $9.97 postpaid.

To join, simply complete the coupon below and mail to the address provided. **Heartsong Presents** romances are rated G for another reason: They'll arrive *Godspeed!*

YES! Sign me up for Hearts♥ng!

NEW MEMBERSHIPS WILL BE SHIPPED IMMEDIATELY!

Send no money now. We'll bill you only $9.97 post-paid with your first shipment of four books. Or for faster action, call toll free 1-800-847-8270.

NAME ______________________________

ADDRESS ______________________________

CITY ______________ STATE ________ ZIP ________

MAIL TO: HEARTSONG PRESENTS, P.O. Box 719, Uhrichsville, Ohio 44683

YES 9-95